"Beautiful s
can be…nic
Kate said.

"As long as we keep things in perspective, we could share fries and face down hungry seagulls together every now and then until the summer's over," she added.

Every now and then was better than nothing, and Brady let his heart persuade him that some of her time was worth the risk, even though he'd be alone come autumn.

Kate grabbed his hand and tugged him toward the end of the boardwalk where the mermaid statue rose up from the edge of the beach. "The ice cream vendor is down here, and I'm not going back to my apartment without some."

She dropped his hand as they walked toward the floodlights illuminating the forlorn mermaid looking out to sea and waiting for her true love to return.

Dear Reader,

Thank you for spending time in Cape Pursuit, Virginia, where the firefighters are tough but tender and the scenery is beautiful. I love the seaside and the sounds of summer, so it's always fun for me to write a book with a beach setting. If you like reading books in order, here are the three books in this series: *In Love with the Firefighter*, *The Firefighter's Vow* and *A Home for the Firefighter*.

Each book features a different firefighter from the Cape Pursuit Fire Department, but they all find a happily-ever-after with a heroine who is someone you might want to have as a friend.

I love hearing from readers, so please send me a note at author@amiedenman.com or visit @amiedenman on Facebook or Twitter. I hope this book leaves you feeling as if you've just returned from a sweet and satisfying vacation.

Best,

Amie

HEARTWARMING

A Home for the Firefighter

—

Amie Denman

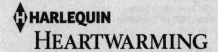

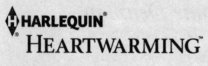

HARLEQUIN®
HEARTWARMING™

Recycling programs for this product may not exist in your area.

ISBN-13: 978-1-335-88976-8

A Home for the Firefighter

Copyright © 2020 by Amie Denman

All rights reserved. No part of this book may be used or reproduced in any manner whatsoever without written permission except in the case of brief quotations embodied in critical articles and reviews.

This is a work of fiction. Names, characters, places and incidents are either the product of the author's imagination or are used fictitiously. Any resemblance to actual persons, living or dead, businesses, companies, events or locales is entirely coincidental.

This edition published by arrangement with Harlequin Books S.A.

For questions and comments about the quality of this book, please contact us at CustomerService@Harlequin.com.

Harlequin Enterprises ULC
22 Adelaide St. West, 40th Floor
Toronto, Ontario M5H 4E3, Canada
www.Harlequin.com

Printed in U.S.A.

Amie Denman is the author of twenty
contemporary romances full of humor and heart.
A devoted traveler whose parents always kept a
suitcase packed, she loves reading and writing
books you could take on vacation. Amie believes
everything is fun, especially wedding cake, show
tunes, roller coasters and falling in love.

Books by Amie Denman

Harlequin Heartwarming

Starlight Point Stories

Under the Boardwalk
Carousel Nights
Meet Me on the Midway
Until the Ride Stops
Back to the Lake Breeze Hotel

Cape Pursuit Firefighters

In Love with the Firefighter
The Firefighter's Vow

Carina Press

Her Lucky Catch

Visit the Author Profile page
at Harlequin.com for more titles.

CHAPTER ONE

BRADY ADAMS DUCKED as a personal watercraft did a swift turn just seconds before it would have hit the fireboat. He caught a glimpse of his friend Charlie Zimmerman at the controls of the personal watercraft and knew a huge wave was coming. The fire chief, who was standing next to Brady, didn't duck, and a cold bath of ocean water meant for Brady hit Chief Tony Ruggles right in the face.

"I could have him arrested for being a public menace," Brady suggested as the chief used both hands to sluice water off his face. "We could make an example out of him as a cautionary tale for all the tourists."

The chief laughed. "I think that's Charlie's motto. If you can't be a good example to others, at least be a horrible warning."

The personal watercraft slowed and came alongside, and Brady noticed the contrite expression on Charlie's face. Dousing the chief with salt water had probably not been the plan.

"Just trying to make it more realistic," Charlie yelled. "The ocean's never this calm and peaceful when we get called out."

Tony shot him a caustic glare. "The new guys on the department don't have much experience with ocean rescue, so when you're bobbing around out there maybe they'll find you before the fish eat you."

Brady smothered a smile and grabbed the line Charlie threw him. He tied the personal watercraft to the side of the fireboat and turned off the diesel engines. He remembered his first time going out on the fireboat and practicing rescue techniques offshore. He glanced at the sparkling white beaches of Cape Pursuit. The tourist town with its huge influx of summer visitors kept the fire department busy but also challenged them to prepare for any emergency on land or water.

"Twenty feet," Brady said, looking at the depth finder on the dashboard of the rescue boat. "Think that's too deep?"

"We're staying on top of the water today," Chief Ruggles said. He grinned as Charlie climbed over the side of the deep-hulled fire-boat. "Being optimistic."

The new members of the department who accompanied them this afternoon had completed some water training in a pool and then in an inland lake, but being on the ocean with waves and salt water was different and more difficult. Brady tossed out the anchor and put on his baseball cap with the logo of the Cape Pursuit Fire Department embroidered on the front. The sun was already hot even though it was only the middle of May.

"What's the plan?" Brady asked.

"We'll toss Charlie in and he can play the part of the struggling swimmer who panics and fights our new recruits all the way back to the boat," Tony said. "After that, we'll move closer to shore and sink the dummy to the bottom and do the human chain search. Water's still pretty cold, but you couldn't ask for a nicer day."

Brady tugged on the straps of Charlie's life jacket and then clapped him on the shoulder. "Good luck, buddy."

Charlie laughed and stepped off the boat. He splashed and flapped his arms in the water and screamed in a high falsetto voice.

"He's not much," Chief Tony Ruggles told the two new firefighters, "but he's got a wonderful wife and a toddler. Better go save him."

The new guys, Hal and Chase, followed their training by checking their own life jackets first and then tossing a life ring to the simulated victim in the water. Charlie ignored the life ring and yelled, "Come save me!"

Hal and Chase jumped into the water and started swimming toward Charlie, who swam away from them in the opposite direction. Brady picked up a long rope with a life ring attached. "I think I could hit him from here," he said, chuckling.

Tony crossed his arms over his chest and sat on the gunwale of the boat. "I knew he'd make this fun for them. That's why I told them Charlie has a wife and child. It makes him a more sympathetic character."

Brady knew the families of all the other guys. He'd been to a few of their weddings and tossed in cash for group baby gifts. Been to some funerals, too. Although the fire department was like a big family, most of the other firefighters were going home to their own spouses and children. Brady's half of a rental house had been empty and silent until a week earlier when his brother and niece had shown up on his doorstep. He loved hearing the water running in the evenings for Bella's bath and having extra dishes in the sink, and he hoped Noah and Bella would stay for a long time. Brady wasn't afraid of burning houses or dangerous rescues, but loneliness got under his skin.

"There you go," Tony yelled, encouraging the two new firefighters. "Hook the life ring to his vest."

Brady forced his thoughts back to the training rescue in the small choppy waves. "Charlie must have gotten tired of leading them on a chase," he said. He laughed as he saw Charlie stretch out on his back, hands behind his head, and float on the water like a big raft, making Hal and Chase work together to drag him toward the boat.

"It would be tempting to jump on that personal watercraft and give him a dose of his own medicine," Tony said.

Brady grinned and nodded. "But you're too nice a guy to do that."

"Correction. I'm too nice to do that to Hal and Chase," Tony said.

An hour later, Brady was at the wheel of

the fire engine on the way back to the station. The diesel noise and the low hum of radio traffic was the background music of his life as a firefighter in the coastal town of Cape Pursuit, Virginia.

"Did I do okay?" the new recruit, Hal, asked. "I've been around boats a lot."

Brady smiled. "I can tell. If we end up going out on a water rescue, I wouldn't mind having you aboard."

He didn't look at Hal, but he knew the twenty-year-old would appreciate the compliment. Brady was only five years his senior, but every day of those five years had been a learning opportunity. Sometimes he thought the fire and rescue service should have no more surprises for him, but each day was still different, demanding and fantastic.

"Too bad we didn't have time for the beach rescue exercise," Hal said.

While they were still on the boat, Tony had heard the radio traffic from two ambulances that were called out on a car accident. He didn't like leaving the station with low manpower even though there were off-duty firefighters and more than a dozen volunteers they could call in. Out of caution, he'd shortened the training exercise, returned to the dock and sent Brady back in the pumper with Hal while the chief drove the smaller rescue truck with Chase. Charlie had driven his own car to the dock where he kept his personal watercraft because he was, technically, off duty and had volunteered to help.

A string of tall hotels with balconies and beach views lined the waterfront in Cape Pursuit, and the strip of road behind the hotels was the flashy area of tourist dining, entertainment and shopping. Restaurants, bars, miniature golf courses, stores selling beach blankets and sunscreen, and upscale shops selling art made the downtown area inviting well beyond the beach. Brady slowed for a tourist on a bicycle who weaved down the side of the street. He wasn't in a huge hurry, and if a call did come in he could flip on the lights and siren. Safety came first, though. Always.

The wandering bicyclist turned at a stop sign, and Brady came to a full stop with the massive fire engine. Facing him at the four-way stop was the Cape Pursuit sightseeing trolley. The glorified bus, painted and styled to look like an old-fashioned trolley car, was a familiar sight in the tourist town. There were several of them, and they ran a daily circuit through Cape Pursuit, providing a way for visitors to hop on and off at hotels, restaurants and several locations along the beach. The longer runs took visitors up the coastline to Norfolk and destinations along the way.

Brady knew most of the trolley drivers and had, in fact, spent the previous summer making extra cash driving one. He was planning another summer of the same trolley shifts mixed with fire station shifts. With another summer of working two jobs, he could finally put away enough savings to make a down payment on his dream of home ownership.

He waved automatically to the driver of the trolley as he always did, but she didn't seem to notice him as she turned to say something to a passenger in the front seat.

It was only a glance.

He could be wrong.

But that driver looked just like Kate Price, who had kissed him and left without a word at the end of the previous summer. There was no way she could be back for another summer…was there?

"CAN I DRIVE?" asked the little boy seated in the first row of seats as Kate pressed the accelerator on the Cape Pursuit trolley after stopping at a four-way stop.

"No, but—"

"Fire truck!" the boy said.

Kate had been about to tell the boy he could ring the bell at the next stop even though she couldn't let him drive the trolley, but she'd been upstaged by a fire truck. She didn't see who was behind the wheel, and it didn't much matter to her. She wasn't back in Cape Pursuit because of a certain firefighter.

She had better reasons.

"How far to the lighthouse?" she heard a woman ask. Kate didn't have to answer because her roommate and coworker, Holly, was in charge of guest relations and narrating the sights and stops along the trolley route. Sometimes they switched jobs and Kate took the role of tour guide, expounding on the history of Cape Pursuit, embellishing a story about pirates and their role in the Virginia town's founding, and making sure guests knew the best place to disembark to get to their destination.

Today, all she had to do was drive the route.

She glanced in the side mirror and saw the huge fire truck retreating down the street.

If Brady chose to work the trolley again for the summer, it would be tough to avoid him. When she'd taken the job, she'd known it was a risk, but the money was hard to pass up now that she finally knew what she wanted to do with her life.

Becoming a flight attendant would give her the entire world to roam and ensure she didn't have to put her shoes on the same mat two nights in a row. But if she wanted to get a job with a good airline, she needed to attend one of the training schools so she would stand out from the other applicants. A great school was housed at the airport, a day's drive down the coast in Orlando, Florida, but it came with a price tag.

With enough hours on the trolley through-out the summer, she could bank the tuition and buy herself the kind of freedom she'd been seeking all twenty-four years of her life.

"Next stop, the mermaid statue," Kate heard Holly say. "It's a great place to enter the public beach, and the pier with shops and restaurants is close by."

Kate slowed the trolley and took a quick glance at the little boy seated behind her. "I could sure use someone to pull this gold chain and ring the bell," she said.

The little boy leaned forward and tugged, and then he giggled when the bell clanged with an electronically simulated old-fashioned sound. Kate smiled. There were far worse ways to earn tuition money than driving cheerful tourists around in a beach town known for its hot sand and fun vibe. The job came with decent summer housing, too, which was a bonus. No lease to sign, no commitment.

More than half the riders on the trolley got off at the mermaid statue stop as Kate had imagined they would. They jostled beach bags as they passed her to climb down the steps at the front of the trolley. Many of the riders paused, made eye contact and thanked her. A few stuffed bills into the tip jar she would share with Holly later. The rest of them shuffled off, their flip-flops slapping the steps, intent on their vacation.

Kate didn't blame them. She was always thinking about where she was going next.

"Did you see him?" Holly asked as she sat on the bench right behind the driver's seat.

"Who?"

"Last summer's romance. Your firefighter boyfriend."

Kate chuckled dismissively and shook her head. "He was not a romance. And definitely not my boyfriend."

"Are we talking about Brady, the tall dark-haired man with the big hero shoulders and smile?" Holly asked.

Kate got up and descended the steps to get off the trolley for a few minutes. Fresh air was all she needed, and maybe Holly would give up the conversation. No luck. Holly followed her off the bus and together they flanked the door. Tourists lined up and showed their trolley passes, and Kate and Holly smiled at them and welcomed them aboard.

"He was driving that fire truck across from us at that stop sign," Holly said. "You had to see him, and he certainly had to see you."

"I didn't notice," Kate said. "I was busy doing my job."

She tried to sound haughty and judgmental of Holly, but Holly just laughed.

"I wonder if he'll work the trolley again this summer. Wasn't he saving his pennies to buy a house?" Holly asked.

Kate boarded the trolley and searched the

small bin of supplies they kept by the driver's seat. She grabbed a roll of stickers with a cartoon trolley on them and went down the center aisle, giving one to each child already seated. She heard Holly greeting riders and smelled the pungent aroma of salty ocean-wet bathing suits and sunscreen. Riders getting on the bus around noon had already put in their beach time and were probably ready to hit the showers and buffet at their hotels.

She sat in the driver's seat and gave trolley stickers to the last children boarding with their parents. Holly climbed up the steps, closed the door and leaned close to Kate to whisper, "This could be your chance to rekindle the flame."

Kate shooed her away with a sweep of her hand. There was nothing to rekindle. She had worked with Brady, gone out with a group a few times that included him and gone to two bonfires on the beach for summer workers. The kiss over Labor Day weekend had been spontaneous and unexpected. For both of them, she'd thought. She'd been quick to assure him it meant nothing, and then she'd said goodbye to Cape Pursuit, her summer job and Brady Adams.

She had nothing to regret, and as far as she knew, he had bought his dream house and carried a bride over the threshold in the long months since she had last seen him.

Kate drove to the next stop, which was centrally located between two large chain hotels on the northern end of the beach strip. Along the drive, she hardly heard the familiar spiel Holly was reeling out over the trolley's speaker system. It was familiar. Too familiar. Maybe she was wrong to come back to Cape Pursuit for another summer. She seldom kept a job for long and loved the feeling of freedom that came with packing up and leaving.

It was the money and steady hours that drew her back to Cape Pursuit. And the tips. The tourist town had filled her bank account enough for her to travel, hike and ski all winter between jobs. One more summer of shuttling beach guests would fund her way to a job that was like a permanent vacation.

Her trolley emptied out at the hotel stop and Holly, once again, appeared beside her, phone in hand. "Have you downloaded the summer employee app? It's going to be fun. The company is running all kinds of incentives and rewards for participating in employee events and team building."

Kate sighed. Getting to know people and risking relationships that would make it tough to move on was something she'd successfully avoided since she left home. Her relationships had shelf lives and expiration dates for a good reason.

"No, thanks," Kate said.

"You don't even know what's on the app. The prizes are pretty tempting," Holly said.

"Let me guess. Cape Pursuit T-shirts and flip-flops?"

Holly frowned. "Those are nice prizes, you know. And they're not the only ones. If you play the ice-breaker games and do other fun things, you build up points for a beach party—"

"We could have our own beach party," Kate suggested.

"And the grand prize is a grand."

"Grand what? Piano?"

"A thousand bucks at the end of the season."

Sunlight glinted off the windshield of an oncoming car as Kate's trolley idled at the beach stop. The light raked her eyes, but it was the thousand bucks that caught her attention. Cash like that meant a larger slice of freedom. Flight attendant school tuition, plus a bankroll while she searched and held out for just the right job.

"Of course the app also has our schedules posted and any updates we need to know about, like weather cancellations," Holly said. "I just pulled up next week's schedule that posted this morning, and guess who's driving the trolley again this summer?"

"Me and you?" Kate said.

"And?"

"Albert Einstein? Martha Washington?"

Holly smiled and held the phone in front of Kate's face so she could see for herself that Brady Adams was on the roster.

"Déjà vu, right?" Holly asked.

"I don't think that's what déjà vu really means," Kate said. "And either way, I plan to keep my mind on my plans and my eyes on the road."

Holly shrugged. "I got a quick look at the guy in the passenger seat in the fire truck. Maybe I'll see if Brady can introduce me. Summer only has one hundred days, and I don't plan to waste them by keeping my mind on my plans and my eyes on the road." She mimicked Kate's tone, and Kate laughed.

"Then I think I'll do the driving and you better keep playing hostess." She handed Holly a roll of trolley stickers and pointed at the line forming outside the door. People with big hats, big beach bags and wiggling kids were ready for an air-conditioned ride on the Cape Pursuit Trolley Line, and driving them was one of the best jobs Kate had ever had.

Holly could laugh, but Kate was determined to stay focused, and that meant keeping Brady at arm's length.

CHAPTER TWO

TWO DAYS LATER, Kate picked up the early-afternoon tourists getting on at the public beach. She'd only been in Cape Pursuit for a week, but the routine was already familiar, just like last year with a few subtle changes. She didn't mind a routine as long as she saw different people every day.

A blonde girl wearing a pink towel over her shoulders climbed up the steps onto the trolley, using both hands to steady herself. Kate smiled at the girl and then raised her eyes to the man right behind her.

Brady Adams. He had a blue towel over his shoulders, sunglasses perched in his wet hair and the same broad grin and broad shoulders as last summer. The child was new.

"Tickets?" Kate asked. The habitual greeting was the only way she could distract herself from the reckless thought that it was nice to see Brady again. And who was the child?

Brady smiled a long, slow smile at Kate and then leaned down and held out his palm in front of the little girl. "You're in charge, remember?"

The girl reached into her purple beach bag and pulled out a spray can of sunscreen, an empty water bottle and a trolley pass. She dropped the sunscreen and Brady caught it in midair. The little girl smiled and gave the trolley pass to Kate.

"Uncle Brady told me I could hold on to it. And I did," she said.

"Your uncle is very lucky to have you to help him," Kate said. Brady was an uncle? She thought she had known more about him than she should have the previous summer and when she'd flirted close to starting a relationship. But she didn't know he had a brother or sister. She smiled at the little girl. "Welcome aboard the Cape Pursuit trolley. I hope you enjoy your ride."

It was her standard line for boarding guests, and Kate was glad to fall back on it instead of asking the questions swimming in her brain.

"You're holding up the line," a man behind Brady said.

Brady grinned. "You can charge my brother double for being a pain in the neck."

A man who was a carbon copy of Brady, but a year or two younger with slightly lighter hair, stuck his head out from behind Brady's shoulder and handed Kate his pass.

"Welcome," she said.

Kate craned her neck to see the line behind Brady's family, and she was relieved when they took the hint and went to a seat.

Except the seat was in the front row where she could already feel Brady's scrutiny. Maybe there was a chance he'd forgotten all about their kiss last September. She risked a glance at him and caught him looking right at her with a question in his chocolate brown eyes.

Nope. No chance.

In all fairness, she hadn't *forgotten* the kiss. She'd just assigned it to a low level of importance in the grand scheme of things.

Kate drove two blocks and tried to tune in to what her trolley partner, Josh, was saying over the speaker. By the second or third week of summer, none of the workers needed the quick reference card with talking points, and Kate tried to listen and memorize the new material. She preferred to drive, but she took the host role sometimes, too, out of fairness.

Josh was giving the weather report and some common-sense warnings about the sun. He moved on to the tide schedule and the useful information almost distracted Kate from the feeling that Brady Adams was right behind her. Almost.

At the next stop, she parked and allowed guests to disembark. Company policy called for a two-minute time delay at the trolley stop even if there was no one waiting and no one in sight. As the summer got busier, there were always guests ready for an air-conditioned ride.

As she waited, with Brady practically breathing down her neck, Kate realized it was going to be a long two minutes unless she took matters into her own hands. Kate swiveled around, fully intending to address the little girl with friendly conversation. Even though she had very little experience with children, Kate reasoned that the little girl would make a safer conversationalist than Brady. However, her plan failed immediately when Kate saw the girl had leaned against her dad's shoulder and closed her eyes. Brady's brother also had his eyes closed.

"I'm awake," Brady said in a cheerful low voice.

Kate took a breath and resolved to conduct a light and impersonal chat. "Are you still a firefighter?"

"Yes," he said, smiling and waiting as if he was going to make her work toward pleasant conversation.

She could turn right back around and ignore him, but she had no idea how long his group would be on the trolley. She could be in for another hour of torture.

"And you're working for the trolley company, too," she said.

He nodded.

Was he really going to make her do all the work? She almost considered bringing up the subject of the kiss and telling him it was seawater under the pier and she didn't want to hear a single word about it.

"You noticed," he said.

She raised an eyebrow.

"That I'm working the trolley."

"Your name is on the schedule on the app," she said. "I saw it on my iPhone."

Brady's smile faded. "Do I have to look online this year? They gave us printed copies of the schedule last year."

"Just download it on your phone," Kate said. "It's easy."

Brady held out his phone.

"Sorry," Kate said. "I have to get the trolley moving."

She skipped ringing the bell because she didn't want to wake up Brady's adorable niece, whose mouth had fallen open in a deep sleep.

"There's usually a long break at the next stop," Brady said. "Maybe you could help me then."

Kate had just been thinking the same thing about the next stop and its longer boarding time and wondering if she should offer to trade jobs with Josh. Perhaps her partner would like to drive, even though it was only his second day on the job. She blew out a long breath and eased away from the trolley stop. There was no need to risk anyone's safety when she was perfectly capable of keeping her thoughts on her own goals. She was the captain of her own ship, and that strategy had been working for her since she was eighteen.

The next stop was in front of a four-corner section of resorts. Each resort had at least fifteen floors and the trolley felt small in comparison. Beach-weary guests bundled off with their towels and bags, and afternoon sunseekers lined up for their chance to board. Kate imagined them going off to lunch in the hotel snack shops or taking cool refreshing showers in their rooms. Travel and vacations were her favorite things, and her nomad life occasionally included a stay in an upscale resort. She kept those stays short so she wouldn't be too tempted to remain longer.

Her funds were bottomed out at the moment, but a summer of taking as many trolley shifts as she could get would put her back in the money and on to her next adventure. Winning the cash prize for participating in the employee social app would be pure bonus. Was there a chance Brady would play along, too, and would that mean—

Kate felt a tap on her shoulder.

"If you'll just find the app for me and get the download started—" Brady's words were much too close to her ear "—I'll fill out a comment card and say your customer service was five-star."

"I'm sure you can manage."

"Usually, yes, but when my brother came to town just over a week ago, we both upgraded to new iPhones. It was a 'buy one get one free' special and we got the family plan. I used to have a much older Android phone."

"Is he working for the trolley company, too?" Kate asked, indicating Brady's sleeping brother.

Brady shook his head. "Noah's not sure of his plans yet, but I'm lucky to have him and Bella staying with me while he figures it out. If you don't want to help me, I could wake up Noah and ask him, but the poor guy's perpetually tired. I had no idea how much energy a four-year-old girl has."

Kate swiveled in her driver's seat, hesitated just a moment as she contemplated one of the few men who'd ever tempted her to want more, and then took his phone. It was better to get it over with, and she didn't want him to have to interrupt his brother's nap. She searched the app store, found the summer worker's app and clicked the install button. She handed it to Brady, but he didn't reach for it.

"Better hold on to it a minute and make sure it works," he said.

Kate shook her head. She wanted to put her hands back on the wheel and move along. "It'll work," she assured him.

"I know," he said, smiling. "I have confidence in you."

And that was just like Brady. Kate was tempted to ask him how he'd been and if he'd fulfilled his dream of buying a house yet, but she didn't. It was too risky to let herself fall into an easy friendship with someone who would expect more. Besides, if his plans had fallen through, he wouldn't want to talk about it. His dreams didn't match hers in any shape or size, but they were his dreams and she respected that. She knew what it meant to want something that was very hard to get.

AFTER BRADY GOT off the trolley at the stop only a block from the fire station, he waved to his brother and his niece as they pulled away. Noah would indulge Bella for a little while yet on the trolley, and then he'd get off at a stop within walking distance of the house they were sharing. Bella's little pink face in the window made him laugh, but the firefighter in him also hoped his brother would wash off all her sunscreen and make certain she drank a lot of fluids for the rest of the day.

Brady was almost jealous that his brother would always have a piece of his heart walking around in Bella, but he was glad he'd get to share at least part of the summer with his niece.

After a quick change into one of the uniforms he always kept in his station locker, he started his shift with an ambulance call to a residence on the edge of Cape Pursuit. Brady and his partner, Ethan, took an older man with chest pains to the hospital and returned to find that the rest of the crew had done the station chores and made dinner. Taking advantage of a quiet moment, Brady enjoyed the evening sunshine while he sat on a bench outside the fire station. He pulled out his phone and contemplated the new icon on the home screen.

"I thought you hated your new phone," Ethan said as he came outside and sat beside Brady.

"I'm making peace with it. My second job has decided to post our schedules online and use direct deposit for all paychecks."

Ethan nodded at the phone. "Are you working a lot?"

"I hope so," Brady said. "I asked George to give me as many hours as I can work around my shifts here."

"Down payment?" Ethan asked, smiling.

"That's the plan."

The firefighters all knew at least something about the personal lives of their colleagues, and Brady had made no secret of his hopes regarding a home of his own. Those hopes had expanded in a different direction since his brother and niece had come to town unexpectedly, and having the chance to offer them a home—even just a slice of his rental house—made Brady's dream both more real and more urgent.

The sooner he could choose, finance and move into his own four walls, the better. For himself, Noah and Bella. Noah's relationship with his girlfriend, Corrinne, was a question hanging in the air and Brady hadn't wanted to press his brother. He knew there had been marriage talk at one time, a separation that went on for several months and now some family emergency for Corrinne that meant she had to trust Noah with their daughter for a month or maybe more.

"Maybe I should get my trolley license," Ethan said.

Brady laughed. "You don't need a special license. And you don't need extra cash, do you?"

Ethan was the quietest and most serious firefighter at the station. Not unfriendly. In fact, he showed great compassion for patients and his colleagues. He was always the designated driver, always had a big-brother ear for anyone who needed it. Brady had confided a few details about his absent father, his single mother and a childhood that could be summed up in the word *uncertainty*. Ethan had listened, nodded and revealed just enough about his own parents to make Brady understand why he never drank and always watched out for his friends.

"My parents haven't made the wisest decisions financially since my dad was…encouraged…to retire early." Ethan forced a smile. "Think they'd let me ring the bell if I drove the trolley?"

"You're overqualified after driving the fire

truck and blowing the siren, but I bet they'd give you a chance."

Brady put his finger on the app button and tapped it open. He read a welcome message from George, who owned the company employing summer workers on the trolley and at several other tourist locations in town. George owned a miniature golf course, a bicycle rental and an ice cream shop on the beach in addition to the trolley.

"This seems either good or bad," Brady said. He held the phone so Ethan could see the screen as he scrolled through the app. "It looks like a summer-long game. You have to participate in all these activities and you win points toward the grand prize."

"What's the grand prize?"

"A thousand dollars," Brady said.

"That's some motivation."

Brady's mind went immediately to his down payment savings account. The money would help a lot, but the online game appeared to be social and interactive. He didn't have a lot of time on his hands, working two jobs.

"Your first assignment is the classic two

truths and one lie game," Ethan said, reading over Brady's shoulder. "You should try it."

"I'm not sure what I'd say."

"I'll help you," Ethan offered. "Two truths would be that you're a firefighter and an uncle. The lie could be something involving your dancing ability."

"That sounds boring," Brady said.

"Say you're a traveling Flamenco dancer and you hire yourself out to parties," Ethan suggested. "Although that would be better if it were true because no one would suspect you did that if they knew you." Ethan scrubbed a hand over his face. "Maybe I'm not very good at this."

"I can't just say the firefighter and uncle part. There are other facts about me, and the point is to not say obvious stuff so you can throw people off."

Ethan leaned back and crossed his arms over his chest. "Maybe I'll pick up some overtime here at the station for some extra cash. It may be easier than playing this game."

Brady laughed. He didn't have to use the app for anything other than finding out his schedule. It would be very easy to shove the phone back in his shirt pocket and forget all about competing for the grand prize. If he didn't get to know the other summer workers, there would be no harm. He'd tried getting close to one the previous year, and it had definitely not worked out.

Kate hadn't changed. She was medium height, but her straight shoulders and the way she carried herself made her seem taller. Her hair was long and straight and appeared brown unless she was in the direct sunlight. He remembered the way streaks of gold wove through her hair one day last summer when they walked along the beach with some of her friends. She still drew him toward her like the sound of a waterfall, but she had doused him with cold water.

He couldn't imagine her playing the app game because forming relationships with other summer workers was clearly not in her travel plans. But she had been the one to tell him about the app. Maybe…

He scrolled through the usernames and avatars, looking for Kate. There were flowers, emojis, race cars and animal pictures with goofy nicknames identifying the summer workers who were already playing. Finally, he found a picture of an airplane with Kate's name under it.

If ever a woman was a flight risk, it was Kate Price. He clicked the avatar and discovered she had entered three items of information about herself. He smiled, intrigued by the thought of sorting the truth from the lies.

I have been to forty-three states. I hate flowers. I am an only child.

Brady considered the three statements. It was very easy to believe Kate had been to forty-three states, but it could be a trick question. Perhaps she'd been to forty-two or even forty-four. It was, quite possibly, an arbitrary number. As for hating flowers, maybe he was old-fashioned, but it seemed unlikely that any woman would hate flowers. Or was that a stupid assumption?

Was Kate an only child? He'd lived just outside her circle last year, intrigued by her and finally kissing her. But he didn't know the simplest thing about her. Was he going to get the chance to find out?

CHAPTER THREE

KATE SAVED THE spreadsheet her boss, George, had left open on his office computer. It was the third day in a row George had trusted her to do his paperwork and added an hour or two to the end of the shift.

He paid her for her extra time, and keeping track of summer workers' time, business expenditures and daily revenues was a simple matter of accurate record keeping and attention to detail. Not the most exciting job she'd ever had, but definitely not the hardest.

She left the office and pulled the door shut behind her. The workers running the trolley on the late-evening shifts all knew the keycode to get into the office in case they'd left personal items in there. The sun had nearly set and the pink light washed the beach and pier with watercolors. George's business office was tiny, but it had a magical location.

Right on the beach by the pier, in the middle of all the action Cape Pursuit offered.

Kate noticed three vehicles in the office parking lot. One pickup truck, one tiny hatchback and one older sedan that looked as if it was borrowed from someone's grandparents. Some employees drove to work, and some took advantage of a free trolley pass for the entire summer, hopping on and off at locations nearest their homes.

The trolley pulled up and Kate climbed the three steps as soon as the door opened. She shared a room in summer employee housing in a dated but clean complex two stops north on the trolley route. She owned a reliable car, but she had already put a lot of miles on it by driving for Uber on and off over the past two years. Taking the trolley gave her car and herself a nice break after a long day at work.

"Hello," a friendly voice said, pulling Kate from her thoughts about getting off her feet and microwaving something to eat. "I'm your courteous trolley driver. Do you have a ticket?"

Brady grinned at her, and Kate laughed. "No ticket. I'm considering hijacking this wagon, so you better take me where I want to go or there could be trouble."

He held both hands in the air. "I'm working alone tonight, so I'm at your mercy."

"Where's your narrator?"

"Went home early to prepare for tomorrow's hangover. I've had three passengers in the last hour, and none of them cared about the narrated tour. I have fifteen minutes left in my shift, and then I'm getting a triple cheeseburger."

"Sounds good," Kate said.

Brady raised an eyebrow. "I'll buy."

"I wasn't inviting myself along," Kate said, shaking her head.

"I don't mind doing the dirty work," Brady said. "Kate, will you please have a triple cheeseburger with me? There may also be fries and ice cream involved. I want you to know that up front."

She had no intention of having a dinner date with Brady, no matter how good fries and ice cream sounded.

"I can't."

"Because you're not hungry?" Brady asked.

"I have plans for a late dinner." It was a very lean version of the truth, but it was technically true. She had frozen burritos and chicken potpies in the small freezer in the kitchen she shared with Holly.

Brady's brow wrinkled, but he nodded. "Have a seat wherever you like."

Kate was relieved he wasn't going to argue and try to persuade her into dinner, even if it was just a burger between coworkers after their shifts. That wasn't a date, but it was a slippery slope she had no plans to tiptoe across.

"You usually work the earlier shifts, don't you?" Brady asked.

With the new summer app, everyone had easy access to everyone else's schedules, so it was no surprise he would know that.

"I did, but then I stayed over a few hours and did some office work for George. He seems to be pouring a lot of effort into his business."

"I noticed that. I hope it's a good sign."

"How wouldn't it be?"

Brady shrugged. "Sometimes people fix things up right before they sell them, but I don't know what George's plans are."

Kate sat in the front seat, not wanting to sit farther back and make Brady think he'd offended her. He closed the trolley door, rang the bell and then handed her the wireless microphone.

"There's no one on board," she said.

"I know. But you could pretend you're entertaining guests with an amusing story about yourself. An anecdote from your lifetime of trolley experience that could change their lives."

Kate hesitated. Brady's playfulness was a giant part of his appeal, and she remembered being surprised to learn the previous summer that he rescued people and put out fires on a daily basis. Weren't firefighters supposed to be very serious?

"Consider it a safety measure. I was out most of the night on calls at the station, so I'm tired and you'd be helping me stay awake and drive."

"Maybe you should let me drive," Kate said.

Brady shook his head. "I'd rather listen. Perhaps you could name your favorite…color or baseball team…or flower."

"I don't—" she began, and then she remembered the three facts she'd entered into that stupid social media app. She'd revealed that she hated flowers, but no one in Cape

Pursuit could know that it was because of the year she worked for a florist delivering flowers. If it weren't for the prize of a thousand bucks, she wouldn't open herself up to anyone's attention.

"Don't?"

"Have a favorite baseball team," Kate said. She'd been about to say she didn't like flowers, but if by some chance Brady had managed to open the first challenge on the app and find her profile, she wasn't going to make it easy for him.

"Want a suggestion for a team or a color?"

Kate sighed and sank against the seat back. One block had already gone by and her stop was coming up in just minutes. She didn't regret her refusal of a burger with Brady, even though it would have been far tastier than whatever her freezer offered up. Dinner was definitely a bad idea, especially with someone so sweet and funny. Kate loved people, but she kept her friendships light and transient. Aside from a few friends she checked in with on social media, she didn't have a lot of ties.

Brady was the kind of man who liked ties.

"I like blue," Brady said. "Almost every

shade except the really light ones. Ocean blue, midnight blue, royal blue. All good."

"Is that one of the truths you put on the employee app?"

He turned his head and grinned at her. "I thought of much more interesting truths."

"And a lie?"

"That was harder, but I'll leave it to you to decide if I really went to ten different elementary schools or not."

Kate laughed. "You seem like the kind of man who likes to be in one place."

Brady didn't answer, but she noticed his hands flexing on the steering wheel. He was probably thinking about what opposites they were. If she had said she'd gone to ten different elementary schools, people would probably believe it readily. But nothing could be farther from the truth. She'd hardly been outside a ten-mile radius in her first eighteen years on the planet.

"Did you get your own house yet?" she asked, hoping the answer would be yes and he would fill the last few minutes of their ride with wonderful, boring details about paint colors, window screens and basement drainage systems. It would be safely impersonal.

"Not yet. That's why I'm back here working for the summer."

Kate absorbed that thought as she looked out the windows at the darkening city of Cape Pursuit. They had passed the bulk of the tourist strip with its hotels, restaurants and bars. Her stop was just one short block away.

"Why are you back?" Brady asked.

Kate let the question hang in the cool air. Brady coasted to a stop and set the brake, but he didn't open the door, which would automatically turn the interior lights on. Kate faced him in the semidarkness, wondering if she should tell him her plans. It was none of his business, but it would make it clear that any ideas he might have about a relationship or a repeat of last summer's kiss would be useless. She'd be moving on as soon as summer ended.

"I'm here for the same reason you are," she said. She got up and Brady pulled the lever to open the door, giving Kate a quick exit whenever she wanted it. She put a hand on the shiny brass railing at the top of the steps. There was no one else on the trolley, and Brady was at the end of his shift. There was no hurry, and she could take the time to let him know her future was already planned and didn't include him.

Brady's stomach rumbled like a long peal of thunder, and he put a hand on it and laughed. "I wasn't kidding about that triple cheeseburger. Working two jobs is definitely cutting into my eating time."

"I don't want to hold you up," Kate said. She put a foot on the top step and the movement brought her eye level with Brady in the driver's seat. It wouldn't hurt to level with him. "I'm going to flight attendant school in September. That's why I'm here. I'm earning my tuition money, and then I'll be all over the world and getting paid for it."

She smiled as the images of Europe, bright blue oceans, Australia, Hawaii and every other beautiful place she'd seen on travel posters rolled through her head. She'd had plenty of time to develop her imagination and her appetite for seeing new places as she crossed the United States in her freight-truck days.

Being a flight attendant would be much more glamorous.

Brady nodded, but his expression clouded

as if he had a question he'd like to ask but wasn't going to. "You'll love that."

He said it quietly, but his words cut right through her. Why did such a simple statement sound like a criticism?

"You're darn right I will," she said as she descended the steps, hiked her bag over her shoulder and headed off to her summer apartment. Brady could eat a cheeseburger and fries all by himself.

KATE SAT IN the last seat on the trolley with the microphone in her lap. Holly was at the wheel. Kate didn't love the way her friend often bumped the curbs at stops, accelerated too slowly and tended to get behind by a minute or two at each stop. But, she reasoned, Holly would get better at all of those things if she drove more often, and it wasn't fair for Kate to grab the seat at the wheel every time. Holly had also worked for the tourist company the year before and had been Kate's roommate, but Holly had worked most of the summer at the bike rental instead of the trolley.

When Holly grazed the curb at the mermaid statue trolley stop at six minutes past three in the afternoon, Kate hopped off and greeted people as they entered the trolley. If she scanned their passes and helped them board quickly, they might make up the six minutes by the end of their shift. She disguised a frown when she saw the sheer number of people lined up to board the bus. They all looked sun-weary with pink skin, salt-water-tousled hair and sandy feet in flip-flops. One man covered his eyes with his hand and pinched his temples.

Beach time was over for the day for this group of tourists. Kate smiled at them and tried to get them onto the air-conditioned trolley as quickly as she could. An older man traveling in a group with who appeared to be his kids and grandkids had a tough time picking up his foot to get it on the bottom step. Kate reached out a hand to steady him, but he had already gripped the railing on both sides of the steps.

"Got a cramp in my leg," he said. "I tried to play Frisbee on the sand with my grandkids, and I wore myself out before I even knew what hit me."

Although it was blistering hot, the man wasn't sweating like all the other guests who were wiping their brows and upper lips with the corners of their beach towels.

"You have to pace yourself," Kate said. "Are you staying in Cape Pursuit for the week?"

The man gave her a confused expression, and she thought she heard him say, "I don't know," as he labored up the steps. Poor guy. He was going to need a vacation from his vacation.

Kate scanned boarding passes and tried to get everyone aboard so they could move along. There would be hot, tired people waiting at the next stops, and one of the hallmarks of the Cape Pursuit Trolley Line was the fact that it promised to run on time. She gave Holly the sign to close the door, gave the bell a quick pull and went to her seat at the back of the bus.

"Thank you for riding the Cape Pursuit Trolley Line," she began in a cheerful voice over the speaker system. "We hope you're all having a wonderful day in our beach town. As you ride in cool comfort to your final stop, I'd like to share some highlights with you. I'm sure you saw the mermaid statue on the beach where you just boarded. You might be interested to know that the statue is much more popular with tourists than with some of the local city leaders. It's rumored that the artist they commissioned to sculpt it chose a more anatomically realistic style than expected."

Kate paused and a few people chuckled, as they usually did. "No matter what you think of the statue, the mermaid looking out to sea and hoping for the return of her beloved sailor is part of the town's history as a sailing port and even a location for pirates to shelter from weather and the law."

The mention of pirates usually got a few heads to turn, but the children aboard the trolley were too hot and tired to show much interest. Kate moved on to narrating the names of the streets they passed, the hotels and even suggesting some of the restaurants. She always made sure to point out the miniature golf course and ice cream stand owned by her employer.

The older man with the leg cramp had taken a seat across from her in the back of the trolley, and she saw him leaning over in his seat. At first she thought he was trying to massage the cramp out of his calf, but then she noticed he had rested his head on the back of the seat in front of him. And he wasn't moving.

Was he asleep? Ill? She saw a lot of hot, tired tourists, but everyone on the trolley staff had also been trained in basic first aid, especially the kinds of problems they might see in a summer beach town. The older man's family had sat in front of him and they were busy looking at pictures on their phones and talking about where they were going for dinner.

Kate put a hand on the man's shoulder and noticed he was shaking. Or was it shivering?

"Are you okay?" she asked. The man barely acknowledged her. "Sir?" she said more loudly.

Kate tapped the shoulder of the woman sitting in front of the older man. She turned and looked and Kate pointed.

"Dad?" the woman asked. "Are you okay?" She hopped out of her seat and squeezed in next to her father.

He turned a confused gaze on her. "Margaret, when did you get back from Europe?"

Kate pulled out her phone and dialed 911. As she spoke to the operator and explained her suspicions about a heatstroke victim, she strode to the front of the trolley. The next stop was in sight, and Kate told Holly to pull up at the stop and empty out all the passengers. On her way back to the ill man, she noticed an ice chest tucked under one of the trolley seats.

"Do you have ice left?" she asked.

The woman shook her head. "My son left it open and our ice turned to water. We poured it out on the beach."

"I have ice," the man two rows behind her said. He pointed to the red plastic rolling ice chest at his feet.

"I've got an overheated man in the back," Kate said. "May I?"

"Sure," the tourist said. "I'll come help."

As Kate and the man with the ice chest made their way to the back of the trolley, she felt the vehicle come to a stop and saw all the people getting off. No one argued or asked questions. Kate propped the sick man on the seat as comfortably as she could. She grabbed a beach towel from one of his grandkids. "Do you have any more of these?" she asked.

"Got some smaller ones in my bag," the woman whom the older man had called Margaret said.

Kate took the towels, filled them with ice

and put the ice packs under the man's arms and on his head. She had his grandkids take a seat toward the front of the trolley so they would be out of the way and, hopefully, not too frightened by their grandfather's appearance. Holly came back after escorting all the guests off.

"What can I do?"

"Meet the ambulance crew when they pull up. I told the 911 operator the emergency was on the trolley and told her what stop we were at, but anything we can do to get this man to the hospital faster will help."

It was only minutes later when Kate heard sirens, but the minutes had been frightening. The heatstroke victim had closed his eyes and his breathing didn't seem right. His daughter Margaret was becoming more and more agitated, but Kate could see she was trying to be calm for the sake of her children sitting in the front of the trolley with their eyes glued on the back.

"What do we have?" a familiar voice asked.

Kate glanced up and was so relieved to see Brady Adams she could have hugged him. Instead, she told him everything that had happened and what she had done. He and his partner listened intently and were already checking the victim's pulse and feeling his skin.

"You did exactly the right thing," Brady said, his voice low and calm. "Can you open the emergency door in the back?"

"Yes," Kate said. The door was within arm's reach and she had it propped open in seconds. Brady and his partner lifted their patient out the door, secured him to a stretcher and rolled him into the ambulance. They worked smoothly together as if it was something they did every day. Kate approached Brady just before he shut the back door of the rescue vehicle.

"I'll arrange for his family to meet him at the hospital," she said.

He nodded and gave her a long serious look. "Perfect," he said.

Kate didn't feel perfect. Now that the patient was in better hands, her adrenaline crashed and left her feeling as if she'd just jumped from a great height and miraculously landed on her feet.

How on earth did Brady face emergencies every day and keep his heart and mind intact?

Maybe having a job like his was the reason he wanted the stability of his own home. For the first time, Brady's dream made sense to her.

CHAPTER FOUR

BRADY TOOK ADVANTAGE of a rare evening off and an even more elusive chance to go out with his friends from the fire department. With coverage twenty-four hours a day, especially in the summer, the Cape Pursuit Fire Department kept its roster busy. And he was more than ready to blow off a bit of steam.

"Not driving the trolley tonight?" Chief Tony Ruggles asked as he got out of a black pickup with his cousin Kevin Russell, who was also a captain on the department. Both men had on jackets with the hoods pulled up.

Brady shook his head. "The rain gave me a bonus night off." It wasn't just rain, it was a downpour, and beach town tourists were either staying in their hotel bars and restaurants or taking Uber if they wanted to venture out. Waiting at trolley stops didn't have any appeal on a night like this.

The Cape Pursuit Bar and Grill had an unimaginative name but a loyal clientele. Just off the tourist strip, the one-story brown building had ample parking that was already filling up even though it was just past six in the evening. Brady assumed the crowd would be mostly locals, people he'd known for years, who would find their way a few streets off the tourist map.

"Did you ever hear how that kid from the accident this morning is doing?" Brady asked the chief as they stepped inside the front door and shook off the rain. He knew it wasn't likely, but he always hoped to hear what happened to people after the initial emergency was over. How did families cope with their burned houses or garages? What happened with that leg injury from surfing? Did Grandpa get to golf again after his heart attack? In such a tight-knit community, Brady sometimes heard about the locals, but seldom the tourists.

"Believe it or not, we got a call at the station from the mom," Tony said. He took a seat at the fire department's usual table just under the big-screen televisions near the bar. "She wanted to say thank you and tell us the boy's going to be okay. May need surgery on the leg, but we minimized the damage by getting him unpinned as fast as we did."

Brady nodded and smiled. Car accidents were always serious, especially when a victim was entrapped. Even worse when it was a child. A rental sedan with tourists had tangled with a carload of teenagers heading to the beach before the weather turned rainy, and it could have been a lot worse. Only the boy in the back seat of the tourist rental had received serious injuries despite how bad it looked when Brady and his partners pulled up with an ambulance and a rescue truck.

"We'll have to drink to that," Kevin said.

They ordered drinks and the standard appetizer—a big plate of mozzarella sticks, wings, fries, onion rings and fried pickles. Ethan, Charlie, Gavin and one of the newer volunteers, Chase, arrived at the same time the plate of appetizers did. All of the new arrivals ordered a beer except for Ethan, who always stayed sober and drove his oversized SUV just in case someone needed a ride. Brady had only gotten a ride home with Ethan one time when he had had too many beers celebrating his twenty-first birthday almost four years earlier.

"How's the trolley service treating you?" Charlie asked. "Get your down payment money ready to go yet? I've got a list of houses to look at whenever you're ready."

"Soon," Brady said. With his part-time job as a local real estate agent, Charlie made it a point of pride to make sure his fellow firefighters saw a carefully curated list of houses when they were in the market. "I'm also trying to win the cash bonus of a thousand dollars at the end of the summer by playing an online game."

"Didn't take you for a gambler," Charlie commented. "Not that I'm judging."

Brady laughed. "Not gambling. Look." He opened the app on his phone and slid it over to Charlie.

"You've already racked up some points," Charlie commented. "My wife would be good at this two truths and a lie thing. Jane knows everyone in this town, even the temporary workers, I swear." Brady could readily believe Jane knew everyone, both as the owner of a local art studio and also as a member of the town council.

"The truth and lies game is almost over," Brady said. "I have some good ideas, but I don't want to waste my guesses because you lose points if you're wrong."

"Who are we trying to figure out?" Charlie asked.

Brady glanced across the bar as a group of people entered. Kate Price and several other women who worked for the tourist company paused and brushed off rain just inside the door.

"I see she's back," Charlie said. Brady didn't have to ask who he meant. He'd been foolish enough to mention he'd kissed Kate at the end of the previous season and the other guys had teased him about it. They'd brought it up a few times over the winter, sometimes with teasing but more often with friendly inquiries about if he'd heard from her. Brady never expected to see her again, and it would be impossible to ignore someone who had ignited a little fire in him the summer before and then walked away, leaving it unattended.

Unattended fires were dangerous.

"Just for the summer again," Brady said. "And then I'm sure she'll disappear."

Charlie looked at the phone app. "You haven't answered the question about her."

Brady shook his head.

"You could buy her a drink and try to bring up the subject."

"I wouldn't take advantage of her like that," Brady said. His feelings for Kate went beyond trickery. Had she thought about him in the long months between September and June? He had finally stored away that wonderful moment from the end of last summer when the new season rolled around and Kate surfaced again.

"Then you could offer her a fair trade. One fact for one fact," Tony said. "No dishonor in that." His grin suggested he wasn't lecturing Brady or speaking as his boss. Tony had found love in an unexpected place the previous summer with one of the volunteer firefighters brave enough to put her life and her heart on the line. Laura had enrolled in firefighting school with the intention of becoming a full-time professional, but she still found time to volunteer at Cape Pursuit. And now Tony and Laura were engaged and planning an autumn wedding.

Brady smiled at Tony. "Maybe I will."

As the firefighters talked about a recent rescue call and a fire from the previous week, Brady kept part of his attention on Kate and her friends. He knew one of the other women in her group, Holly, who also worked on the trolleys. The company had several tourist-related businesses, although the trolley one was the largest, so Brady didn't know all the workers in town for the season. A few had returned from the previous year, but it was mostly a transient group of college students looking for a carefree summer job and some tuition money.

When he finished his beer, Brady got up and went over to Kate's table. To his surprise, she glanced up with a smile. "I was hoping to talk to you."

She was?

"Can I ask how the man with heatstroke is doing or is that violating some privacy law?" she said. She slid out from her booth and stood in front of Brady. For a moment he thought she wanted to be close to him, but then he realized it was more likely so she didn't have to talk loudly over the bar noise. Brady noticed her companions went on with their conversation as if nothing had happened. Kate seemed different from the other summer workers. She was the same age as he was, a fact he'd managed to learn about her the previous summer, so she was a bit older than the college students.

"Come sit with me over here for a minute," he said, motioning toward a quiet end of the bar where two stools were unoccupied.

"I think the heatstroke patient will be okay," he said once they were seated. "It was really a good thing you noticed what was happening and called us right away. Heatstroke can be fatal if it gets away from you."

"The poor man," she said. Her expressive blue eyes were wide and sad, and Brady wanted to take her hand and assure her everything was fine. Kate seldom showed vulnerability, and Brady found it undid his resolve to keep his distance even more than her beautiful smile and sense of humor.

Kate's appeal had so many layers he was afraid to even start peeling them back, knowing he would just find himself lonely and hurt again when the season ended.

"We started an IV and pumped fluids into him all the way to the hospital, and they're no strangers to heatstroke at the Cape Pursuit Medical Center. We see probably a dozen cases a year. If you catch it fast enough, people usually recover quickly."

"I'm so glad," she said. "I felt terrible for his family."

Brady wanted to ask her about her own family, which she never mentioned, but he didn't dare. It was too nice having her attention to risk pushing her away by being nosy. He was happy to take any scrap of friendship she was willing to spare for him because he found her fascinating, a puzzle he'd like to decode.

KATE GLANCED OVER at her table of friends, who were enjoying their food and drinks.

"Did you need to get back to your friends?" Brady asked. He dipped his head and leaned closer so she could hear him. "I'm sorry to drag you away."

Kate shrugged. "It was my choice. I'm glad to hear about our trolley guest."

"Want something?" the bartender asked, his smile friendly and patient. "Drink?"

Brady gave Kate an inquiring look, but she shook her head. "No, thanks."

"Nothing for me right now, Bob," Brady said. He turned back to her. "I'm sorry, is your drink getting warm over at your table?"

Kate wondered if Brady was trying to get

rid of her. Did he want her to go back to her friends? Even though she didn't want to get drawn into anything romantic with him, she liked Brady and didn't mind sitting with him.

"No," she said. "I had my one drink—my limit—and I was just hanging out making sure my friends don't get in cars with strangers."

"Would they?"

"One of them might if she drinks too much. Holly doesn't always think twelve hours ahead like she should."

Brady glanced at his watch. "In twelve hours, I'll be at the station for a twenty-four-hour shift. Maybe I don't want to think about that, either."

"But at least your day will be exciting, right? You must have a lot of interesting stories." Kate didn't like the idea of being tied down to one town, but she admired the bravery of the firefighters and their pulse-pounding job. Each day had to be different, and she could almost talk herself into a job like that. Becoming a flight attendant would offer her new views every day and there was no way to get tied down to one place when she would seldom be on the ground.

Brady laughed. "Believe it or not, there are some days that are so quiet and boring we had to install a basketball hoop on the concrete apron at the station just to have something to do."

"That's terrible."

"Actually, it's really good. If we're bored, then people are safe. And we get to stay in shape and humiliate our friends in dunking contests."

Kate smiled. "So you're good at basketball."

Brady shrugged and propped an elbow on the bar. He smiled. "I had to do something to fit in at those ten different schools I attended."

Kate cleared her throat. "Such a skill might have helped me out in those forty-four states I visited."

"I thought it was forty-three," Brady said.

"Ha, I caught you. Trying to cheat?"

"Absolutely. I'm afraid I don't stand a chance against some of the players who only have one job this summer, so I'm trying to earn points where I can."

Kate sighed. "I'm pretty busy, too, and definitely not as inclined to get involved in the personal lives of the other summer workers."

"So we could help each other," Brady said.

Kate considered the offer. Winning the grand prize would be nice, but she didn't think her chances were very good. Earning points was only half the battle, though. Everyone who earned at least one hundred points would be entered in the drawing, so it would come down to equal parts hustle and luck. Kate did not consider herself a lucky person and had battled her own way to everything she'd achieved since she left home at eighteen. Getting help from someone was strangely comforting and appealing but also unsettling. Would help make her feel beholden, controlled? All the people she'd known growing up had beefy bank accounts, trust funds and inheritances to boost them into life. Those were some of the things she was escaping.

"Are you a self-made man or did someone help you get where you are?" she asked before she even had time to consider the strangeness of her question.

Brady laughed and leaned back on his bar stool. He stared at her for a moment. "As a low-wage firefighter and public servant, I've never been asked that question before."

"Sorry," she said. "Forget I asked it."

"No, I can answer it easily. I've struggled every step of my life. Absolutely no one helped me but myself."

It was hard to believe he'd struggled. He was tall, handsome, cheerful, successful. Brady Adams seemed like the kind of man who had always been followed around by sunshine.

"Don't believe me?" he asked. "I'll tell you an honest truth and you're welcome to use the information. I did go to ten different schools before I graduated, none of them by my choice, and most of them I'd like to forget."

Kate drew in a quick breath. There was a lot she didn't know about Brady. She'd tried hard not to get involved with him, but his integrity was hard to miss, even from the safe emotional distance she'd tried to keep. She wanted to say something caring and thoughtful. Had he endured a miserable childhood? Was it awful always being the new kid? Did someone pack his lunch and make sure he had a jacket? She should offer sympathy, but it was much safer to simply give him a fact in return. How could it hurt?

"I've visited forty-five states," she said. "And my only regret is that there are five I haven't gotten to yet."

Brady pulled his elbow off the bar and his expression sobered. It was still kind, but no longer jovial. "That's a big difference between us, Kate."

Loud laughter rang out from the table where Kate's friends sat and Brady turned around to look. "Who's that guy?" Kate asked, pointing to a broad-shouldered young man standing next to her friends' table.

"Chase. One of our new guys," Brady said, turning back to Kate. "He seems like a decent guy, although I don't know a lot about him except that he's anxious to learn fast and he loves boats. I think he's going to join our water rescue team."

"Are you on that team?" It sounded dangerous to Kate, and it suddenly struck home to her that Brady must put his life in danger often in the interest of saving other people. All the firefighters did, but imagining Brady rushing into a burning building or diving into the dark waters of the ocean to save someone made her wish she was brave enough to get to know him better. How had a boy who moved around constantly as a child turned into a man who spent his life rescuing others?

Brady nodded. "Almost all five years I've been on the department."

The more she learned about Brady, the more questions she found herself with. She'd always assumed Brady was from Cape Pursuit and had grown up in a perfect house somewhere in town. He just seemed the type. Of course, she had grown up in what appeared to be a perfect house, a gardened and tastefully decorated prison where her mother was happy to stay inside the walls. *Can we go to the park, Mom? Wait until your father gets home, princess.* That had been the pattern of her childhood. And usually, by the time they had a polite dinner eaten off good china, her mother decided it was too close to dark to go out, even if Kate promised not to get her clothes dirty.

"Are you from the Cape Pursuit area?" she asked, curiosity getting the better of her. It would do her no good to get interested in a person she would never see again when the summer season ended.

Brady's smile faltered, and he considered her question for a few seconds before answering. That alone told Kate the answer to what should have been a simple yes or no question.

"It's home now," he said. "And if I'm very lucky, my brother and my niece will stay, too."

Did the adorable niece have a mother? Why was Brady's brother apparently staying with him?

More laughter from the table she'd abandoned interrupted her thoughts, and she saw the waiter deliver two pitchers of beer to her three friends. "I better go," she said. The new firefighter had squeezed himself into her spot in the booth and was pouring a round for the three women.

"Are things getting out of control?" he asked. Brady glanced over his shoulder. He swung back around and smiled at her. "I think I'll grab Chase and haul him back to my table if you don't think your friends will mind."

"They might mind," Kate said, pressing her lips together.

"I'll tell him the chief wants to talk with him about coming in early tomorrow. That will get his attention and get him out of your seat."

"Thanks. I owe you one. I'd tell you I'm an only child and I hate flowers, but I'm sure you already figured out those are true."

"Why do you hate flowers?" he asked, his voice dipping low and his attention focused on her as if she were the only person in the bar.

"Long story."

Brady nodded. "Something to look forward to."

He got up, walked over to the table where Chase was loudly telling a story to the three ladies and leaned down to say something in Chase's ear. In seconds, they were both on their way to the table by the television where five other men sat.

Brady was a good friend to have, Kate thought. Just a friend.

CHAPTER FIVE

SEVERAL DAYS LATER, Brady picked up Charlie for a round of house showings that had Brady nervous, but excited. He couldn't have high hopes with his firefighter salary and his meager down payment amount so far, but his heart beat a little faster than usual on the sunny morning.

"I see you brought some helpers along," Charlie said as he got in the truck and saw Noah and Bella buckled into the narrow back seat.

"Second opinions," Brady said. He was glad his brother was interested in going along because Noah was probably the person who understood him the most. They'd been together through all the upheavals as kids, and had huddled together in meager twin beds in a cold new place more than once. "Noah just finished his associate's degree in accounting, so that also makes him my financial adviser," Brady added.

"Your flat-broke financial adviser living with you rent free," Noah said, laughing.

"It's good that you came along," Charlie said. "I think I've got some houses on the list that you're all going to love."

"Anything is going to look good compared to the apartment I shared with a bartender and a musician for the last year," Noah said from the back seat. "So I'm easy to please, but my daughter has excellent taste."

Brady heard Bella giggle in the back seat, and it reminded him how important it was to be able to offer her a home for as long as she and his brother needed it.

"Are any of these potential houses in my budget?" He hated sounding like a broken recording, but Brady wanted to be honest with his friend instead of wasting his time on pipe dreams.

"Most of them are close," Charlie said. He leaned forward in the front seat of Brady's truck. "Turn right up here, next street."

Brady put on his turn signal as instructed, but he was already worried. His budget and dreams didn't usually match the beach-town prices of homes. Especially in the summer when the appeal of living in Cape Pursuit, Virginia, right on the Atlantic Coast, was not lost on potential home buyers. Visitors were known to purchase available homes and turn them into rentals for most of the year except for a few weeks when they came to enjoy the houses themselves. Brady had been in Cape Pursuit for eight years, and it seemed to him that the town had grown and gotten nicer with each year—and prices had gone up to match.

"It's the one-story with the big tree in the front yard," Charlie said. "You can park in the driveway because it's unoccupied. Owners already moved out, which is a plus for you since they'll be anxious to sell and you could move in whenever you want."

Brady's heart and enthusiasm sank. It was too nice. The roof was in excellent shape, the siding a nice light blue and there was a front porch that someone had bothered to dress up with an overhang and a decorative railing. It even had an attached garage. No way was it in his price range. He turned off the engine as he parked in front of the wide garage door.

"I know what you're thinking, but give it a chance," Charlie said. "It's just a little bit

outside your range, and like I said, the owners might negotiate."

Brady got out of the truck, unwilling to
give up before he saw the inside. His rental
house had been adequate for Brady, but it
didn't offer the permanence he was looking
for. The family in the other half of the duplex was generally pleasant, but hearing their
television through the wall and smelling their
cooking reminded him that the home wasn't
his. And having Bella and Noah living in the
two-bedroom, one-bath space made it pain-
fully clear it wasn't large enough.

He and Noah had finally had a conversation the night before about his brother's status.
Bella was four years old and, so far, hadn't
lived with both her parents together. Noah
hadn't known about her for the first year of
her life because his former girlfriend, Corrinne, had thought he was too immature to
be a dad to her child. When they'd met again
and rekindled a romance, Noah had the surprise of his life waiting for him. But Brady
was proud of his brother's attitude and adjust-
ment. He wanted to be a great father, and he
was trying hard. Coming to Cape Pursuit and

living with Brady while looking for a steady job was evidence of his maturity.

Having Bella for the summer while Corrinne focused on a serious family illness was the ultimate test, and so far Noah was passing the test. With help from Brady. If Corrinne agreed to let Noah share custody of Bella, he would need a place to live, and Brady wanted to give them both a permanent home so Bella wouldn't have to grow up as Brady and Noah did.

"Wow," Bella said. "It's pretty."

Brady and Noah exchanged a glance, and Noah gave him a quick pat on the shoulder.

Brady walked up to the front door, determined to at least give this house a try. Already, he could picture Noah and Bella living there with him. And if Noah could get a decent job in Cape Pursuit…could they put their money together and give Bella the childhood she—every kid—deserved?

"I don't want to scare you away," Charlie said as he unlocked the front door, "but it even has a pool in the backyard."

"A pool," Bella squealed, and then Brady heard Noah explaining to his daughter that they were just looking and not to get too excited about anything.

Brady groaned, knowing a pool would drive up the price, but also imagining his niece splashing around, learning to swim, having her friends over. It was too good to be true.

When Charlie opened the front door and let Brady go in first, Brady's first impression was spaciousness. Wide laminate flooring and natural light combined with the emptiness made it seem as if anything was possible. Even his shabby couch and chair and scarred coffee table would look better in such a perfect living space. He could have them recovered, work on refinishing the table himself on his days off.

"Three bedrooms, a full bathroom and a half bathroom right down this hall," Charlie said, pointing. "Whenever you're ready."

Three bedrooms. One for him, one for Noah and the sunniest one for Bella. *If only.*

Bella tugged Noah's hand and led the way down the hallway. As they stood in the first bedroom, its emptiness made it look giant.

"Nice windows," Noah said. "I love how bright this place is."

They exchanged a glance and Brady nodded. He knew what his brother was thinking, remembering the various small houses where they'd lived, one after another. The one thing they always seemed to have in common was the smell and the darkness. Curtains closed over small windows as if there was something to hide or hide from.

Brady let out a long breath as Bella ran in to report that one of the other rooms was painted pink.

"You can have that one," Noah teased his brother, lightening the mood.

They looked through the rest of the rooms and made a circuit of the backyard. When they were ready to move on to the next house, Noah buckled Bella into her seat and then came around to the driver's side where Brady stood looking at the light blue house for a moment more.

"Too good to be true, right?" Noah said quietly.

"Maybe not," Brady said. He'd always tried to shelter Noah, but he knew his brother could see just as well as he could that the house would be on the very far reaches of affordability.

They had time to look at two more houses before Charlie had an appointment with another client. Although Brady doubted any house could compare to the first one with the light blue siding, one of the other houses also had him imagining life with his brother and niece, all together, securely putting down roots. The second house was a two-story on the edge of town away from the desirable beach district, but the price reflected its location. It had a fenced-in yard with a playset, and there were two bathrooms in addition to three bedrooms. Bella hopped on the playset's swing and Noah indulged her by pushing her while Brady went through the house with Charlie.

The third house was well within his price range, but it only took ten seconds for Brady to know it wasn't the place for him. The floors were spongy and there was graffiti painted on the back wall near some neglected trash cans. Located on an alley, it reminded him of some of the stomach-churning places he and Noah had stayed when their mom was between men and houses. Even the smell of the house had the stench of neglect, indifference. Noah stepped inside, took a brief lap around the living room and kitchen and then picked up Bella and went outside.

Brady joined Noah and Bella with Charlie five minutes later and found his brother sitting on the tailgate of the truck with Bella on his lap. He was letting Bella play a game on his phone and she seemed absorbed in rearranging colorful shapes.

"Couldn't do it," Noah said, shaking his head.

"Me neither," Brady said. "That one's definitely out even if they gave it to me."

Brady dropped Charlie off at his realty office and Noah and Bella off at home, and then he drove straight to the trolley station where he was planning to make some extra money on his day off from the fire department. It was June 10, and the city of Cape Pursuit was planning its official Kick Off the Summer event. The summer tourist season had already started, but each day brought more tourists. Cape Pursuit took advantage of every precious day of the season to promote its offerings and show tourists a good time so they would return for their next vacation.

"Am I driving or narrating?" he asked when he swung onto the trolley and found

Kate with a clipboard doing a pre-work-check. Her long dark hair was in a ponytail and she had her sunglasses perched on top of her head as if she was ready to take on a long day.

"Your choice," she said as she looked up and smiled. "I almost grabbed the driver's seat because I don't usually like to ride with anyone else, but you're a good driver."

"Thanks." Her praise gave him a little glow of happiness that almost erased the pit in his stomach from the last stop on his tour with Charlie. Something about that place had taken him back to being eleven years old and wondering where his next school was going to be. Worse yet, he remembered trying to make himself and Noah as small and quiet as possible so they stayed under the radar. He'd always thought being saddled with two young boys was the reason why their mom never seemed to find a new husband.

He knew better now, but the old insecurity felt fresh again. Working at the fire station restored his self-confidence every day, and even driving the trolley gave him a sense of purpose and ability to direct the course of his own life—something he'd been doing since he took that high school diploma from a principal whose hand he shook but whose name he'd never even known.

"If you'll give me the other page, I'll do the outside check," he offered. This was his world, and it was just like the fire department. Check the turn signals, headlights, tires. Make note of any dents or scratches. Sign off and start driving. Of course, the daily checks of the fire trucks were a lot more complicated, but this was still familiar territory.

"Already did it," Kate said. "I got here early."

"Sorry," Brady said automatically. He wasn't late, but he didn't like arriving just in time and leaving the prep work for someone else. Especially Kate.

"No problem," she said, smiling at him over the clipboard. Brady's heart responded to that beautiful smile, and he was secretly thrilled that he would get to spend the next eight hours working the same trolley with Kate. He didn't care that it would be an outrageously busy day as long as she was there, too, and he could hear her voice over the speaker and glance over his shoulder at trolley stops just to see her.

"Hey, Kate, you in there?"

Brady recognized the voice of their employer, George, a second before the man poked his head inside the door of the trolley.

"Oh, good, you're here, too," George said, pointing at Brady. "I need my best two drivers in the driver's seat today, so I'd like to put Kate on the blue trolley and have you on the red one here."

"Sure," Kate said quickly.

Brady smiled and nodded, disappointment running through him like a cold drink. Was Kate as disappointed to get assigned a different partner for the day as he was?

"I'll find you both a narrator," George continued, "and I know you two will keep the trolleys moving on schedule unlike some of the drivers who meander and lose time at each stop. We need to run smoothly today."

George disappeared and Kate handed Brady the clipboard. "It's all done," she said. "You're ready to go."

"I wish I was working with you," he said, trying to keep his voice neutral and friendly.

She tucked loose strands of hair behind her ears and cocked her head, looking at him for a minute before she said anything. "You're the most dependable coworker I have," she said. "Must be the firefighter in you."

Brady swallowed and stepped closer to take the clipboard. He paused with his fingers on it, enjoying a moment of indirect contact with her. "I'd be dependable no matter what I did for a living," he said.

She didn't answer, but he already knew that a solid dependable existence wasn't exactly what she was looking for. He watched Kate board the blue trolley and was about to head over and help her with her precheck, but Josh clambered aboard the red trolley.

"Hey, fire chief," he said. "Looks like we're partners today and George told me we better get moving."

Brady smiled at the teenager. "I'm not the fire chief, just a lowly public servant."

Josh laughed. "I'll call you captain, then. Makes you seem cool."

If only Kate thought he was cool, Brady would happily drive the trolley until the sun set and rose again over Cape Pursuit.

KATE LOVED DRIVING. Loved the thrill of being in control and going somewhere, anywhere. However, after a solid eight hours behind the wheel of the trolley with only a brief break somewhere in the middle of the long sunny day, she was ready to hand over the keys for the day. The Kick Off the Summer event was great. She remembered loving it the year before. At that time, she had no plan for her future and didn't know where she'd be when the tourist season ended.

This summer was different. With a plan in place, she wouldn't have to spend another fall, winter and spring moving from job to job. She was going to train for a job that allowed her to fly all over the world but also offered her—she shuddered to even think the word—stability. Stability without suffocation. She could have one without the other... couldn't she?

"I'm done," Brady said, leaning in the door of her trolley. "I must have driven a million tourists to the moon and back today."

"At least," Kate agreed. Her shoulders were tight and her eyes were tired, and she knew Brady must feel the same way. His trolley was parked right next to hers at the trolley office near the beach, but another driver would hop in the driver's seat for the late-night tourist run. The after-dark tourists were usually adults who were enjoying the bars and night-life. Kate was not sorry to be missing that group of tourists after a long day of celebrat-ing summer, and she imagined Brady would be just as glad to hand over the keys.

"I think everyone in this town has had fun today except for us," Brady said, echoing her thoughts.

Kate laughed. "It's fun driving the trolley."

Brady nodded. "No doubt, but I'm think-ing of taking off my nametag and my shoes and joining the party."

"Don't you think it's dangerous walking around with no shoes? I thought you were a guy who erred on the side of safety."

"I am," Brady said. "But I'm cooling down my feet in the ocean for a few minutes before I go eat something I'll regret later. Would you like to join me?"

"With the regret?"

He shook his head and smiled at her as he stood framed in the door. She was still in the driver's seat, key in hand. While he waited for her answer, he took off his nametag and put it in his pocket. He wore navy-blue shorts and a red Cape Pursuit Trolley Company T-shirt, the uniform of the summer trolley staff. He propped a foot on the lower step of her trolley and untied one shoe, removed it and then did the same with the other. He stuffed his socks into the shoes and untucked his shirt.

"You look like a tourist now," Kate said.

"Thank you. Your turn."

This was starting to feel personal, which usually made alarm bells ring in Kate's head. Getting personally involved with someone else was the first loop in a long series of ties.

"I'll be out in a minute," she said, hoping he would take the hint and step away from her door.

"I'll wait." He walked over to a bench near the trolley office where he could get a clear view of the ocean.

Kate's relief driver, who would take the late shift, hopped on, clipboard in hand, and Kate handed him the keys. She offered to help him with the checklist on the clipboard, but he turned her down. She took off her nametag and untucked her shirt, enjoying the feeling of freedom that came with it. Kate crossed the narrow parking lot and sat on the bench with Brady.

"You're still wearing shoes," he observed.

"I have to clock out, and the floor in the office is sticky."

Brady handed her his company identification card. "Would you swipe mine, too?"

She took the card and headed into the small office. Kate swiped hers first and then Brady's, and then took a closer look at his card. There was a picture, and he was smiling. Of course. The man seemed to have a permanent smile. It was one of the things she had noticed about him first. *What did people notice about her first?*

In addition to the picture, the card had his name and his birth date, which also doubled as the employee number. Brady had a birthday later this summer, she noticed. He'd be twenty-five a few months before she turned the same age in November. It was a personal detail she didn't have a right to know, but he had handed her the card without reservation.

When Kate returned to the bench, Brady held out his large hand, palm up, and she laid the card in it while being careful not to touch him. He was like one of those beautiful desserts behind glass at a bakery. So tempting, but so not good for her. She was afraid to even take a close look for fear of being drawn in.

She should leave her shoes on and walk herself right over to her car. She glanced at Brady, but he wasn't paying any attention to her. He was staring at the ocean's edge, tension radiating from his body. "Do you hear that?" he asked.

She directed her gaze toward the ocean and listened. Someone was screaming and she thought she heard the word *help*.

Brady was off the bench and running before she could answer his question. Kate peeled off her shoes and socks and left them next to his, and then she raced across the sand right behind him. There was no way she could catch him, as his legs ate up the distance faster than a train, but then he suddenly stopped.

Kate bumped into him and knocked them both over. Brady sprawled on the sand, hand over his chest, laughing. Kate scrambled up. "What happened?"

"False alarm. I realized when I got close that it was just kids goofing around, yelling for help but they were fine." Brady sat up, still breathing heavily. "I hate it when people do that, but my brother and I acted like fools, too, when we were kids."

Kate sank to the sand next to him. "I haven't run that fast in a long time."

"Or knocked anyone over?"

She laughed. "That, either."

Brady leaned back on his elbows. "Now that we're both shoeless and I'm suddenly starving, should we go to the Kick Off festival? We deserve a treat."

Kate shoved around a little hill of sand with her fingers and let the sand slide between them. It felt cool and refreshing and the sunset streaked the water pretty colors. It was as if someone had packaged a summer evening, and for a brief moment she wanted to stay in Cape Pursuit and keep the summer exactly as it was.

She shook off that unexpected thought and tried for a casual tone. "Why not?" she said, even though seeing Brady's handsome face right next to her reminded her of all the reasons why she shouldn't.

CHAPTER SIX

HIS HEART STILL raced and his limbs vibrated from adrenaline from that cry of help that had him racing across the sand. His brain had registered it as a false alarm but it took his feet a while to get the message and slow down. Being barreled over from behind by Kate was almost the last thing he expected. Was she planning to help somehow? He didn't doubt her bravery, but she was also a person who didn't get involved in other people's lives. At least, she had been the previous summer, but something about her seemed a little...softer... this summer.

"I heard people talking about french fries half the day and then I had to smell all the ones tourists brought on the trolley with them," Kate said.

"So, no to the fries?"

Kate laughed and gave him a little tap on the upper arm. "Yes to the fries. It's been kill-

ing me all day. And we might as well start
with the food trucks in the park and then
work our way down to the mermaid statue
on the boardwalk. That's where the home-
made ice cream vendor is set up, according
to about two hundred people who got on my
trolley talking about it."

Brady liked the sound of this plan. Given
the crowds, lines and distance from the park
to the other end of the boardwalk, he could
count on at least two hours of Kate's time.

"You're a fast runner," Kate said.

"Only in short sprints," Brady admitted as
they picked up their shoes and then walked
the length of beach to the park entrance. "I
like playing basketball, but if I tried to run
a mile straight, I'd probably need an ambulance."

"I like hiking," Kate said without elabora-
tion. A clue to the mysterious hidden life of
Kate Price?

"Was that what you were doing in forty-
seven states?" he asked.

"Forty-five."

"Close enough."

"I hiked when I could, but a lot of my time
was spent behind the wheel."

Brady was tempted to take her hand. They both carried their shoes as they walked the beach, but he planned to find a bench when they got to the grassy park and put his shoes back on.

"Don't tell me you've driven a trolley across the United States and back, narrating all the attractions along the way," he said.

Kate turned to him with a smile. "Worse. I was driving a freight truck."

"Filled with flowers? Is that why you hate flowers?"

"The flowers were a different job. That was three years ago in New York City. You can't believe how many flowers get delivered to weddings and funerals every day. And the smell clings to you no matter how long you stand in the shower and try to wash it off."

"Flower smell can't be that bad," Brady commented.

They entered the park and Brady motioned toward a bench where they sat side by side, almost touching, and pulled on their socks and shoes.

"I like wildflowers," Kate said. "But the hothouse ones bother me. They're grown to perfection in little glass-walled prisons, and when they are just about to be perfect, chop," she said, mimicking scissors with her hands. "Chopped and shipped. Heck of a way to live and die."

Brady was afraid to say anything aloud, but he believed he might be getting a glimpse into Kate Price that left him with more questions than answers.

Kate popped up. "Fry truck," she said, pointing. She started walking and Brady had to finish tying his shoe and catch up with her. He slipped into line next to Kate, hoping she might resume telling him about her experiences driving freight and flowers and hiking. She was fascinating, but elusive, like a beautiful butterfly you couldn't catch.

"It's a better deal if we get the large and split it," she said, her attention focused on the menu on the side of the food truck. A woman with a large order of steaming fries left the window and walked past them.

"Now I'm dying," Brady said. "We could cut in line."

Kate laughed and looked up at him. "You wouldn't do that."

"No, I wouldn't. But it's tempting."

"I thought I would never look at another

french fry after driving a truck all over the country for a year," Kate said. "Fast food is lousy, but sometimes it was the only choice."

"What did you deliver in your truck?"

"Anything. I worked for a freight company after I got my commercial driver's license. I thought it would be a great way to see the country. And it was," she said as she moved up a space in line, "but that company got bought out by a hazardous materials shipper, and I thought that was my sign to move on."

They made it to the window and ordered the large carton of fries.

"I delivered pizzas for a few months when I was a senior in high school," Brady said.

"Did you get tired of the pizza smell lingering on you?"

"Not really. I love pizza. But the car I was using got... Well, it wasn't available any longer, so I had to give it up."

He'd almost told her about his mother's boyfriend at that time who ended up taking off with the ancient beat-up car his mother had somehow acquired. He and Noah had learned to drive and taken their license tests in that car. Brady had been almost eighteen and Noah was sixteen when they got their licenses together, taking advantage of the one car their mother had managed to hold on to. Brady had vowed he'd buy a new one with a part-time job, but the money was always needed for something else—like a decent winter coat for his mother and school supplies for his brother.

Even though he had stopped talking, Kate was focused on him as if he was explaining something in great detail. She was watching his face, and he was afraid he'd revealed too much.

"You must have really liked that car," she said with a faint attempt at a smile. "Or the pizza."

Brady swallowed and brought back his usual cheerful expression. "Mostly the pizza." It was a beautiful summer evening, and he was with a woman who intensified his belief that finding someone to be with and put down roots with was the path to happiness. He wasn't going to spoil the mood by telling Kate that his mother had drifted aimlessly when he and his brother were growing up. Only now that he and Noah were grown up and their mother had developed a chronic heart condition did she settle in one place—

with her sister, who was kind enough to take her into her home in a Florida trailer park.

It wasn't a dream life for his mother, but it was better than her previous existence… even though he'd wanted to believe he and his brother brought her some happiness all those difficult years. If she'd only had a solid home, it would have been so much easier for all of them to be happy.

"Large fry," the teen at the window said, and Kate practically leaped forward to grab her order before anyone else did.

"Bench or walk?" Brady asked.

Kate ate a fry and offered the carton to Brady. "We could walk," she said. "I'd like to hear the band on the boardwalk and see what's in all the festival tents down by the mermaid statue."

Brady liked the idea of walking the beach with Kate, even though each step would bring them closer to their destination and the end of the night with her. Just being with her felt like a bonus because he hadn't expected her to return to Cape Pursuit for another summer, and he hadn't expected her to agree to a night out with him. He shouldn't get his hopes up, but…

Kate stopped by a vendor with bottles of soda and water in giant ice chests. She handed over a five-dollar bill and grabbed an orange soda. "I'm buying," she said to Brady as she pointed to the ice chest. He selected a bottle of water and tucked it under his elbow so he could open it with his free hand while still holding the fries. Kate smiled at him and took a handful of fries and then continued walking along the crowded boardwalk. Families, groups of friends and lovers holding hands wandered along the ocean, no one seeming to be in a hurry.

A boy on a skateboard zipped in front of Kate and she stopped short, throwing up her hands as he nearly knocked her over. During the split second her hands were in the air, a seagull swept down and stole the french fry clutched between her fingers. A woman near them shrieked in surprise, but Kate laughed and turned to watch the seagull flying away. Brady wanted to chase down the skateboarder and give him a lecture about safety, but Kate was unharmed and smiling broadly.

"Lucky bird," she said.

"Because he got a fry?" Brady asked.

Kate shook her head. "No. Because he can

fly. That must be amazing to have freedom like that and be able to take off anytime and anywhere you want."

Brady shuddered and worked the cap off his bottle, one-handed, for another cold drink.

"You don't like birds?" Kate asked.

"I'm not crazy about flying," he admitted.

"Did you have a bad experience on a flight?"

"No. No experience at all. I'm just not sure I'd like the feeling of leaving the ground," he said. "I don't mind feeling the earth under my feet."

"You've never flown?" she asked. Her tone implied that he'd never *lived*, and it reminded him how different they were.

He'd been lucky to get a ride to school growing up, and since then he'd relied on a nice sturdy pickup truck, a fire truck or the fireboat to get him where he needed to be. "I never flew as a kid, and I haven't had any reason to since. I've been on a few nice vacations, but you can drive to a lot of places pretty easily from the Virginia shore."

Kate unscrewed her bottle of orange soda and took a long sip as they continued walking the boardwalk. Just ahead, there were food vendors mixed with carts selling souvenirs and glow sticks. Loud music from a band set up on the beach emanated from just ahead, and most of the people on the boardwalk seemed to be heading toward it.

"Did you fly a lot when you were a kid?" Brady asked. Was that part of her obsession with staying on the move and part of her reason for wanting to be a flight attendant?

Kate laughed. "Never. I stayed in one place, went to one school, and my childhood bedroom was still painted the same color the last time I went home."

To Brady, that sounded like a wonderful way to spend a childhood, but Kate's tone and expression made it clear that she didn't think so. They paused at the painted railing that divided the boardwalk from the beach and listened to the band. It was a loud mix of drums and electronic/techno music. Brady wouldn't have tuned his pickup's radio to music like that, but he was willing to listen to it just to be with Kate. People on the beach were dancing and the crowd continued to grow as he stood side by side with Kate and fought the desire to slip an arm around her. It would make a perfect evening even better if he could just feel her against his side and let her long hair tickle his arm when the ocean breeze stirred her dark locks.

When the song finally ended after ten minutes of what sounded to Brady like the same thing over and over, Kate stretched up and her lips brushed his ear. "I don't love this music," she said. "Do you?"

Brady smiled and shook his head, delighted at the feeling of her lips on his ear and the sudden camaraderie he shared with Kate.

"Want to move along?" she asked. Her hand was on his upper arm as she balanced herself with the crowd jostling around her. Brady nodded and surrendered to his feelings as he slipped a protective arm around her. She didn't resist, and they moved away from the people and noise.

As soon as they got to a darker and more secluded part of the boardwalk, Brady removed his arm, knowing he didn't have a good excuse or any right to touch Kate, no matter how much he wanted to pull her close and feel the night air whispering over them both. As soon as he broke the contact between them, Kate glanced up quickly. Was she disappointed? Relieved?

Brady cleared his throat. "Are you glad you came back for the summer?"

"Very," she said quickly.

Was she trying to tell him something?

"I love nights like this, and the smell of the ocean at night. I'm making a nice salary, and it's really going to help this fall," she added.

Brady stopped walking. Kate took another half step and then stopped also, turning to face him. A few people walked past, but their section of the boardwalk was quiet and Brady didn't feel bad taking up the middle of the walkway. He needed to ask Kate for clarification, needed to know if there was anything left in her heart from the previous summer. "Are those the only reasons you're glad to be in Cape Pursuit?" he asked.

Kate looked out to the ocean, and Brady imagined she was thinking about flight, as she always seemed to be. He'd gone too far, and he was probably going to pay for it. To his surprise, though, he saw her shake her head slowly from side to side in the dim light. "It's nice seeing you," she said, her voice low and inviting.

Brady's chest constricted and he willed himself to be calm—something he had practiced while suiting up on the way to a fire or other emergency call. He could breathe deeply, focus and deal with life and death matters while watching out for himself and his partners on the department. He could handle a conversation with a lovely woman under the inky postsunset sky without making a fool of himself or blundering irredeemably.

"Summer is only about a hundred days long," he began, reaching for a rational argument for why she might consider spending her time with him. "And we've already used up a few weeks," he continued, "but there's a lot left."

Kate nodded and, even in the darkness, he could see that she was standing perfectly still, almost holding her breath. He wished he knew what she was thinking.

"And we could enjoy the rest of the summer together," he said. "Without any strings attached if that's how you want it."

In answer, Kate touched his cheek and brushed a quick kiss over his lips. Brady had no idea how to interpret her wordless action, so he kissed her back and it made one fact perfectly clear to him: the memory of last summer's kiss had not been overrated. And this kiss was going to be even harder to forget than the last one. Even though he was the one to suggest a no-strings relationship, he wasn't sure he could downplay the way her lips felt under his.

Kate pulled back and cocked her head, observing him. "That was a test," she said.

Brady almost choked. "I didn't even get a chance to study. Did I pass?"

She laughed and put a light hand on his chest where he was sure she could feel his heart thundering below the surface. "That kiss was just as nice as the one last summer," she said, her voice just a whisper over the sound of the waves.

Brady waited, letting Kate drive the decision. If she told him to go away, he'd walk her to her car and say goodbye. She would probably be doing him a favor since he had a very hard time keeping his feelings on a surface level when Kate was involved.

"Beautiful summer nights like this can be…nice…with someone else," she said. "As long as we keep things in perspective, we could share fries and face down hungry seagulls together every now and then until the summer's over."

Every now and then was better than nothing, and Brady let his heart persuade him that some of her time was worth the risk, even though he'd be alone come autumn.

Kate grabbed his hand and tugged him toward the end of the boardwalk where the mermaid statue rose up from the edge of the beach. "The ice cream vendor is down here, and I'm not going back to my apartment without some." She dropped his hand as they walked toward the floodlights illuminating the forlorn mermaid looking out to sea and waiting for her true love to return.

Brady didn't mind that Kate had let go of his hand. He would have plenty of good thoughts to hold in his heart when he went to bed that night. For a second, he imagined Kate curled up next to him in that beautiful living room he'd seen that morning with his Realtor. But then he made himself be realistic and remember that he'd just agreed to a summer *something* with no strings. He would have to be content with that.

CHAPTER SEVEN

KATE HEARD HER phone chime with a text. She had the day off, and she had a lot to think about. Two nights ago, she had—sort of— agreed to a short-term summer romance with Brady Adams, one of the most appealing men she'd ever met. She wouldn't admit to him or anyone that she'd thought about their September kiss more than once throughout the long winter she spent driving around.

She looked at the name on her screen, almost expecting it to be Brady asking her to spend the day with him. They had already planned to see each other at the employee beach party that night.

The text wasn't from Brady. It was her boss, George, instead.

Call me, please?

Instead of returning his text, Kate tapped the phone button and heard George's voice five seconds later. "First of all, thank you for calling me on your day off. I know those are rare during the summer," he said.

"I don't mind," Kate said. She really didn't. She'd never had a boss who treated her as if she were a human being. Driving freight or flowers or the many other temporary jobs she'd done to get by and preserve her independence had not come with the luxury of respect from employers. "Do you need help with something?" she asked.

"Too much," he said, his voice sounding tired and defeated. "I was fine running the trolley service and bike rental last year without any real office staff, but now that I've added an ice cream parlor and a miniature golf course, I'm over my limit of organizational skills."

Organizational skills was something Kate had more than her share of. Her mother had organized every moment of Kate's day, and every item in the house in its place. Colored pencils had a special cubby and they had to be lined up in it. Her clothes were coordinated right down to her socks and underwear. Even her book bags for school were chosen the night before to complement her jacket, the weather and which matching top and skirt her mother had laid out in her closet. Some girls would have loved such attention, but Kate had found it stifling. Despite her abhorrence of being tied to such lockstep thinking, she had absorbed enough skills for keeping things in place to be useful.

"What can I do for you?" she asked. "I could work in your office today and help get things arranged for the party tonight. Everyone is really looking forward to it."

"What was I thinking?" he groaned.

Kate laughed. "I'll be there in half an hour."

She had already showered and brushed her hair back into a ponytail with the intention of going for a walk and trying out one of the new restaurants in downtown Cape Pursuit that she'd heard tourists talking about. With her spare time, she also planned to pop into the stores and boutiques she usually drove past. Wherever she had traveled across the country, she'd taken some time to enjoy the local culture. Otherwise, she had reasoned, what was the point of traveling?

KATE PUSHED OPEN the office door near the beach and found her boss with his elbows propped on paperwork and his head in his hands. She had already taken on part of the computer system, but George needed help with filing, employee paperwork, ordering supplies and managing the work schedules. She wondered if his secretary, Elena, had the day off or was just falling behind.

"You're a lifesaver," he said. "I have to go to a meeting downtown with the chamber of commerce. You can use Elena's desk."

"Sure," Kate said. "Where's Elena?"

"Quit. Got a better offer in Virginia Beach. She said she'd stay two weeks if I insisted on it, but I didn't want to stand in her way. Her parents live there, and I know she wanted to be closer to them, so I told her to go ahead. She left two days ago."

"That was nice of you," Kate said. She tried to imagine what it would be like to have parents she wanted to live closer to. All she could picture was getting sucked into their neatly ordered and suffocating world.

"It was stupid. I thought I'd be fine until I got a replacement." He tilted his head and gave Kate a serious look. "Would you consider replacing her?"

"No," Kate said, shaking her head quickly. "I'm not a huge fan of being tied to the office, even though you're great to work for." She didn't want to sound ungrateful or make her boss out to be an ogre. "I just really like driving and the freedom of the road."

"You're not really free since you're on a predetermined route and a tight timetable," George said.

"True. Maybe I just like driving," Kate said.

"Well, if I can't persuade you to give up the trolley, at least I appreciate your help today. I know you have some clue about the computer system, and you're not afraid to take charge if you have to. I'll be back around two this afternoon. And thanks, Kate."

When he was gone, Kate started with the piles on his desk. If his office had gotten this out of control in just two days, there was no time to lose. The phone rang with a message from one of the trolley drivers who was calling in sick for the evening. They were already stretched thin on staff because most employees were planning to attend the beach party, just as Kate and Brady were.

The trolley had to go on its route as scheduled because tourists were expecting it. They'd paid for their trolley pass, had plans, needed someone to shuttle them safely home from the bars and beaches. Kate used the former secretary's computer and pulled up the roster of employees, searching for the evening schedule and a possible replacement. Even as she searched, the sinking feeling that the replacement would be her settled over her.

Instead of immediately thinking about the extra money she would make, she thought of the disappointment in Brady's eyes when he found out she wasn't going to the party.

And that was exactly why getting into a relationship with Brady—with anyone—was a bad idea. Freedom to make her own decisions was the driving force in her life, and tying her time and interests to anyone else gave her a flashback of the life she'd abandoned. She pictured her mother saying, "I'll have to see when your father gets home. I couldn't say," whenever anyone invited her to anything. Kate's dad was a nice man, loving even in his own way, who never cheated on his wife, as far as Kate knew, and never failed to pull his gray BMW into the garage at exactly the same time every day.

She glanced at her watch. It was ten o'clock on a Tuesday. Her mother would be at the local grocery store getting a newspaper and a chicken to roast. She didn't trust newspaper delivery after the *New York Times* had shown up late twice and wet once. Kate's dad read the paper while her mother finished dinner. Every night. No matter what.

Sorry, she texted Brady, I have to drive the trolley tonight so I won't be able to go to the beach party. I hope you enjoy it.

She thought a message would ping into her phone within a minute, and she set it next to her computer so she would hear it when it came.

An hour went by, and she had heard nothing from Brady. Not that she had been checking or anything. Her work schedule, her day, her life, did not depend upon his approval or his opinion.

But still. She wanted to know if he had received her message. Would he go to the party, anyway, without her? Ask her to skip out on trolley driving? Tell her he'd find someone else to go with who was prettier than she was and far sweeter?

That last one was so out of character for Brady that Kate almost laughed. She tried to forget her phone and concentrate on untangling whatever system Elena had used to organize employee records and work schedules. It wasn't a typical spreadsheet, but once Kate found the passwords to unlock it written down on the desk calendar, it all began to make sense. She planned to have it at least partially decoded and organized before two o'clock when George returned.

At noon, she grabbed some cash from her bag and locked the office door so she could make a quick run to the sandwich shop on the edge of the beach. Kate got a turkey sub, chips and a drink, knowing it might be the last food she saw that day if she went straight from George's office nightmare to the late shift driving the trolley.

When she returned to the office, there was a message waiting on her phone.

Sorry I just saw your text. Was out on a fire. Want me to bring you food from the party?

She immediately pictured Brady wearing his helmet and gear, fighting a fire. Had they saved a person, a building? Were they all okay? She had lived somewhat dangerously crossing the country dozens of times by herself, but Brady's job was a different kind of danger. She almost texted him to ask if he was okay, but that would be crossing a line she was already teetering on.

She read the third sentence of his message again. So he was going to the party without her? Good. That showed he wasn't going to be clingy or difficult, exactly what she meant when she agreed to a short-term, no-strings relationship. And he was offering to bring her food while she worked. Very friendly and nice. Considerate and polite.

It was just the kind of response she would have wanted...so why was she a little sad that he was cheerfully going to the party without her?

THE FIRE HAD been out for an hour. Brady had spent most of the previous sixty minutes cleaning the hose, restoring the trucks to ready-status and pondering how he should respond to Kate's message. He had glanced at his phone while he rode back to the station with his friend Kevin Russell at the wheel, but he didn't respond right away. He knew very well that his gut response, his first response, would be a big mistake because he wanted to either ask her to choose their date over work or offer to take the trolley shift in her place so she could go to the party. She'd been working hard, and he thought she deserved a night off.

Kate wouldn't like him interfering with her work or her life. He had been filled with hope and excitement after their kiss on the boardwalk two nights earlier, but the reality of having a relationship—even a temporary one—with someone who didn't really want a relationship had sunk in during the hours since.

And so he had settled on the kind of friendly response he'd send to anyone—one of the guys at the station, his brother, the mechanic who serviced their fire trucks once a month. He put his phone on the top shelf of his locker while he cleaned and stowed his coat, pants, boots and helmet. To his surprise, she responded before he even got the coat on a peg.

He was not surprised at her message.

Thanks, anyway, but I'll be busy.

Of course she would be busy, she was driving the trolley. But he knew every timed stop and it wouldn't be that hard to take her some dinner even if she said she didn't want him to.

Brady finished his shift at the fire station with several hours to spare before the evening beach party and cookout. He went home, showered and sat at the tiny kitchen table with his brother while Bella watched a princess movie in the living room next door. With such a small rental house, it was easy to keep an eye on the little girl because she couldn't be very far away.

"Any luck with the job search?" Brady asked.

Noah shoved a résumé toward him. "Will you read this over? I'm nervous that there's some comma out of place and I won't get the job and my child will starve."

Brady laughed. "I don't know all the comma rules, but I do know Bella will never starve while either one of us is alive."

"I'll take her a bowl of crackers while you look that over," Noah said. He poured a bowl of fish-shaped cheddar crackers and took it to his daughter. Brady heard them talking over the princess singing on the television, and he tried to block it out and focus on his brother's résumé. He noticed the permanent address

Noah listed was Brady's rental house. For his little family, the modest half of a ranch house was as permanent as he could provide at the moment, but his dream was getting closer all the time, he hoped.

That evening, Brady put on shorts and a summer T-shirt. He parked in the beach lot and crossed the sand in his flip-flops. He almost skipped the party, but he needed to eat and the promised barbecue was tough to resist.

He was also hoping Kate might have a change of plans and show up, too. Brady scanned the dozens of people on the beach already loading up plates of food or playing volleyball. He recognized nearly all of them and knew their names. Kate's friend Holly sat with three guys on a beach blanket. She looked happy and relaxed, and he wondered how much Kate worried about her friend and if Holly really did make such bad decisions. Even though Kate was reluctant to get involved with people, she behaved like a true friend to Holly.

"Glad you could make it," George said when Brady lined up at the buffet with his plate. The food had been brought in and set up on tables under a tent, and the aroma was just as tempting as Brady had imagined. He'd missed lunch while out on an emergency call, and then decided not to eat much when he got off work, saving his appetite for the party.

"Thanks for having this for us," Brady said. "It's nice being appreciated."

"Couldn't do it without you. I just hope you'll keep coming back every year, because I've got some plans for expanding and I'll need good people."

Brady wanted to ask about the expansion plans, but he didn't want to pry into George's business. Did Kate know about these plans? She'd been spending time on and off in the company office.

"Unless the fire service suddenly starts paying us millionaire salaries, you can probably count on me for next summer's roster," Brady said.

George clapped him on the back and walked away.

Brady filled his plate, found a place to sit and talked with one of the summer workers he knew. Marty was the son of one of the older firefighters on the department. He'd just graduated from high school and was trying to decide on his future. Brady remembered being eighteen and knowing he had to figure things out for himself because there would be no one to help him.

"College or the circus?" Brady asked as Marty finished off a can of soda and tossed it into a recycling bin.

"Your guess is as good as mine. I never thought I wanted to be a firefighter like my dad, but I don't want to sit in a classroom or get stuck in an office."

Brady stretched his legs out and crossed his feet at the ankles. "It's a big world with lots of choices."

"How did you decide to be a firefighter?" Marty asked. "Was your dad in the fire service?"

Brady shook his head. "No." It wasn't the time or place to tell Marty how lucky he was to have firefighter Bill Sherman for a dad. The kid probably already knew it. "You'll figure it out soon, and until then, driving the trolley's not a bad way to spend the summer."

"I'm getting more food," Marty said. "They seem to have plenty."

Brady glanced toward the food tent. Marty

was right. No one was going to go hungry. He thought of Kate driving the trolley, possibly by herself. Everyone else seemed to be at the party. Did she even have a narrator tonight? Someone to give her a break while she got something to eat?

He got up and went to the food line. "Can I get a plate to go for one of the workers who couldn't get the evening off?" he asked.

The woman serving up barbecue sandwiches nodded. She produced a roll of aluminum foil. "Fill a plate and I'll wrap it up for you."

Brady piled up everything he thought Kate might like, and the server wrapped it tightly in foil. He picked up a bottle of water and an orange soda and headed for his truck. He knew the trolley route by heart, and if Kate couldn't come to the party, he would take the party to her.

He caught up with the trolley on the north side of town, one of the farthest stops where tourists could hop on and off. The stop was a newer five-story hotel that advertised great rates and a pool. If no one was waiting to board, it would be a fast stop, so he would have to act quickly.

Brady pulled off the road, grabbed the package of food and the two drinks and ran to the door of the trolley just as it was closing. He thunked on the door with his elbow and it opened.

"Ticket?" Kate asked.

Brady smiled and held out the plate of food. "Will this work?"

Kate glanced at the food and the two bottles in his hand. He didn't know what he'd expected—would she thank him with a kiss or tell him he was the best no-strings brief romance she'd ever had?

"You didn't have to bring me anything," she said. "I'm fine."

Brady let out a long, slow breath. "I know you're fine. I'm just dropping this off in case you have a long night and no breaks."

Kate got out of the driver's seat and took the wrapped plate. Brady tucked both bottles in the cup holders built into the dashboard of the trolley. He noticed there were two couples on the trolley, both of them sitting in the middle rows. If they wanted to, the passengers would overhear anything he said to Kate.

"Thanks," she said. "But I have to go. Schedule to keep, you know."

"I could ride along with you and keep you company," he offered.

Kate shook her head and her expression was back to the focused, fearless one he was accustomed to seeing on her. Where was the playful Kate from a few nights ago, the one who had kissed him on the beach? Had something changed?

"You go back to the party," she said.

"I'm not going back."

"You should."

Did she want to get rid of him?

"I mean, I know you work hard, and you deserve a fun evening," she said.

"Everyone does."

Kate shrugged. "It's fun driving the trolley, and I'm getting paid overtime. Every mile gets me just a little closer to flight attendant school. Can't complain about that."

Brady swallowed and nodded. His goal had been to make sure Kate got something to eat, and he'd accomplished that. She had a schedule to keep, and he had a promise to keep—a light summer romance with no promises beyond September 1. He owed himself and Kate the courtesy of saying good night.

"I think we're on the schedule together tomorrow," he said. "See you then."

On his way home, Noah called his cell phone and Brady picked it up on the second ring. He hated talking on the phone while he drove, but he didn't think his brother would call him if it wasn't important.

"Are you near a store?" Noah asked.

"I could be." Brady had just passed a local grocery he usually shopped at, but he was willing to turn around. "What do you need?"

"Chocolate milk. I'd run out and get it myself, but Bella is already in her pajamas and I hate to drag her out."

"No problem. I'll get it and be home in ten minutes."

Brady put on his turn signal, turned around in a hotel parking lot and went back to the grocery. Maybe Kate wasn't impressed that he'd chased down the trolley to deliver her dinner, but he was important in the eyes of his brother and his niece. He had to keep his feelings for Kate in perspective and remember the people who wanted to share his dream of a secure home and family. In a few months, Kate could be anywhere in the world, but he hoped his brother and niece would be tucked safely under the same roof with him.

CHAPTER EIGHT

THE NIGHT HAD been far too short. Kate had gotten back to her apartment at nearly midnight, listened to Holly talk about the beach party for half an hour and then lain awake for another hour wishing she hadn't dismissed Brady so abruptly. He hadn't been needy, hadn't asked her to put his feelings ahead of her work and had, in fact, been darn considerate and thoughtful.

But the scary realization earlier in the day that she cared about his feelings and worried about his reaction to her decision to skip their date in favor of work had bothered her. Remaining free of emotional ties was her way of staying in control of her life. Granted, Brady didn't seem like the kind of guy who would want to control her. He wanted something else from her—her attention and...affection? If she gave those things, it would be temporary only.

As she pulled her Cape Pursuit Trolley visor a little lower to battle the sunrise coming off the Atlantic, Kate wasn't surprised at all to see Brady cheerfully bounding down the three trolley steps. He carried a clipboard and smiled at her.

"I got here early and hogged the precheck all for myself," he announced. "You don't get to check the tires or sweep under the seats. Sorry."

Kate laughed. "I'm so disappointed."

"Me, too. I was looking forward to at least wiping smudgy fingerprints off the windows, but whoever drove this buggy last night must have cleaned up before it got parked in the trolley garage."

"It was a slow night," Kate said.

"I offered you company," he replied with a smile. "But you were all business and completely resistant to my charms."

"Fine," Kate said. "You're allowed to be charming for the next eight hours since I'm stuck working with you, Mr. Sunshine-in-the-Morning."

"Just for that, I'm letting you drive."

Brady swept out a hand toward the door of the trolley to indicate she should board first.

Kate took the driver's seat, Brady rang the bell and they rolled toward the beach pickup, the first stop on the day's trolley line. It was just eight in the morning, but there were already people dotting the beach with colorful sand buckets, beach towels and totes.

No one was waiting to get on the trolley at the beach stop, but Kate knew the boarding areas in front of hotels and along the tourist strip would be filled with beach-goers waiting for a ride. Brady sat right behind her, the only passenger on the first short leg of the day's route.

"I wish we served doughnuts on the route or had built-in time to stop and get some," he said. "I'm already having a great day, but can you imagine how much better a jelly-filled doughnut would make it? Or maybe cream-filled."

Kate laughed. "You're making me hungry."

"Did you eat the dinner I brought you last night?"

She nodded. "I had a little bit at each stop until I suddenly realized it was all gone. I drank the orange soda, but I put the bottle of water in my fridge for another time. Thanks. It was really sweet of you."

She heard his fingers drumming cheerfully on the seat behind her. "I'm a public servant," he said, "warding off emergencies of all kinds, including food."

"What about the current doughnut emergency?"

"I haven't given up hope," he said.

Kate stopped the trolley in front of a block of tall hotels and she opened the door. Brady got out and greeted the customers, checking their tickets.

"Good morning," Kate heard Brady say. "You picked a perfect day to go to the beach."

Three guests boarded and found seats, wedging their beach bags at their feet.

Kate hopped off the trolley and stood next to Brady. His enthusiasm was contagious. Brady pointed to a man's hat that identified him as an army veteran. "Thank you for your service," Brady said.

"Were you in the military, too?" the man asked. Kate could see the logic in the question. Brady was tall, broad-shouldered and confident.

"Firefighter," he said. "This is my part-time job."

"Be careful out there," the military veteran said. "Dangerous job."

Kate glanced over at Brady, who was offering a hand to a little boy following his mom up the trolley steps. The mom had a baby on one hip and a huge bag on the other shoulder. "There you go, little man. Help your mom pick a good seat."

Kate considered herself an outgoing and friendly person, even though she always felt she had gotten a slow start on being social because of her mother's reluctance to leave the house. Her first day of school—albeit at a small, private one—had been an eye-opener. Still, she had traveled and worked with people so much that she felt at ease talking. However, she couldn't hold a candle to Brady, who seemed to radiate friendliness. He had a giving personality. Kate watched him hold an older man's beach bag while he dug through his wallet for his trolley pass.

Brady deserved the love of someone truly wonderful, and it was a sharp stab to Kate's heart when she remembered there was no way that someone could be her. She wasn't willing to give her heart to anyone, and no way would someone like Brady take love in half measures.

"Ready to roll," Brady said, smiling at Kate when their line dwindled to no one.

Kate followed him onto the trolley and took her driver's seat. She secured the door, put on her seat belt, checked her mirrors and rolled into traffic.

"Welcome aboard, friends," Brady said over the speaker system. "We have five stops between here and the first beach drop-off, but I promise you I'll give you plenty to think about on the way."

Kate knew every inch of the route, but she still had plenty to think about. A tiny sliver of her wanted to attempt a real relationship with Brady, and the rest of her wanted to cut him loose and stop making him think there could be anything lasting between them. Not that he'd asked for that, she reminded herself.

"First of all, a little bit about the city of Cape Pursuit. You may have read the brochures or tuned into the tourist channel on the hotel television."

Several people laughed and Brady chuckled. "I see some of you know what I mean. It's a bit on the cheesy side, but the scenery looks great no matter what. In case you're wondering how the city got its name, it goes back several hundred years to a pirate legend. Do I have any pirates on board?"

Kate knew the script by heart, and Brady was mostly sticking to it, but he was improvising and making it a lot more fun.

"Raise your hands a little higher," he said. Kate glanced in the mirror and saw Brady was pointing at a few kids with their hands up. "Look out for those pirates, folks. Like I said, a pirate gave the city its name when he tried to come ashore to hide his treasure and see his true love. When he was chased away, it's said that he hid his pirate loot along the shore somewhere, but no one has ever found it."

Kate heard some murmuring among the passengers at the tale. People loved hearing it, and the lure of buried treasure was a perennial favorite.

"You may have seen the mermaid statue on the beach," Brady continued. "She looks a bit sad, and that's because she's waiting for her true love, the pirate, to return."

"Maybe she's just sorry she missed out on

the treasure," a man in the front row suggested.

Brady laughed. "That's not the romantic version of the story, but I can see your logic."

Kate stopped the trolley at the next group of hotels and restaurants, and she and Brady repeated the ticket checking and welcoming at the door of the trolley. Brady picked up the microphone as soon as the trolley left the stop.

"Welcome, new riders. I'm happy to present you with two choices for your entertainment for the next six to eight minutes. I could recite the entire history of the great state of Virginia from memory, or you could help me with a little game I'm playing. So, show of hands for history." He paused and Kate heard silence behind her. "How about the game?" She heard sounds of assent and saw hands raised when she glanced in the mirror above her head.

"Okay," Brady said. "Those of us lucky enough to run the trolley also have a chance to play for a big prize at the end of the summer by completing tasks. We find out the challenges by looking at the app on our phones. Here's this week's challenge—I have to do something that will make another employee's day."

Kate wanted to turn around so she could see Brady's face, but she had to keep her eyes on the road. Was he joking around? She hadn't looked at the new challenge that was scheduled to post that morning. Make someone's day?

"You see the excellent driver behind the wheel keeping us all safe on the way to the beach?" Brady said. Kate could feel all the eyes in the bus on her. What was he doing?

"That's Kate, and she's my favorite person to work with. What could I do to make her day? I'm taking suggestions."

Kate breathed in and out slowly, not letting Brady grab her interest or distract her from her job.

"You could send her flowers," a woman's voice suggested.

"Hmm," Brady said. "I wonder if she'd like that?"

Kate knew Brady knew she hated flowers, but it was nice of him not to reject the woman's idea.

"Candy," a child's voice suggested.

"Always a great idea, but you have to know

if someone is a chocolate lover or hates nuts or likes the colorful sugary stuff."

"That's risky," a man said. "You should just tell her she has a nice smile and she makes your day."

Two women sighed, and Kate decided that man knew a thing or two about relationships.

"Kate," Brady said, his voice deepening to a comic announcer voice. "You have a beautiful smile, and you totally make my day."

Kate shook her head as she heard laughter behind her. She put on her turn signal, pulled over and opened the door. As they disembarked, at least one woman and two men smiled and winked at her, and Kate couldn't decide if she wanted to ask her boss to fire Brady or promote him to PR staff for the trolley line.

"Where does all the cheerfulness come from?" Kate asked Brady as they stepped off and welcomed a new group of tourists.

Brady shrugged. "I'm a big guy, plenty of room."

Kate smiled and told guests to watch their step.

"And I have a secret," Brady said quietly.

Kate froze. He wasn't going to reveal his

deep feelings for her, was he? That would be
a disaster.

"I never lose faith in my fellow man, no
matter what."

"Even when people disappoint you?" Kate
asked.

"Especially then," Brady said.

Kate couldn't decide if that was good or
bad, because she already knew she was going
to disappoint him by leaving at the end of the
summer and probably never looking back.
She wanted to ask him what would make his
day, but she already knew. A permanent home
and, she guessed, someone to share it with
him.

THE NEXT DAY, Brady had the morning off from
the fire station and he agreed to take care of
Bella while his brother went to a job interview. He loaned Noah one of his two neck-
ties as well as his pickup truck. It was raining,
and the defrost didn't work on Noah's aging
car. Brady didn't want his brother getting in
an accident because of fogged-up windows
on the way to an interview.

Bella, perhaps sensing her dad's nervousness, was more restless than usual. It was a

warm summer rain, so Brady put up a big umbrella, got Bella into a pair of boots and took her for a walk, hand in hand. They strolled downtown, Bella pausing to splash in the puddles along the way. Brady didn't try to stop her. Splashing in puddles was one of the perks of childhood.

They stopped at a bakery and bought two large chocolate chip cookies, eating them at an indoor table while the raindrops ran down the front window. As they left the shop, the trolley pulled up on its regular route.

"Ride," Bella said, pointing excitedly at the trolley.

"Okay," Brady agreed. He didn't have any other plan for entertaining her on a rainy day, and he didn't know how long his brother would be at his interview. If it took Noah a long time, it was probably a good sign. He checked for text messages from Noah before they boarded the trolley, but there was nothing.

They dashed through the rain and got to the trolley just before the driver closed the door.

Kate.

He wasn't surprised. Kate worked a lot, as many hours as she could get.

"Nice day for ducks out there," she said, pointing at Bella's yellow boots with ducks painted on them.

"Quack," Bella said.

Kate smiled and looked up at Brady. "Did you lose your truck?"

"Loaned it to my brother, and we're out for a fun day while Noah goes to a job interview at the bank."

Kate nodded in acknowledgment, and Brady sat with Bella in the front seat across the aisle from the driver. A young couple was already sitting in the seat right behind Kate, and they looked as if they were so in love they didn't even know they were on public transportation. Brady noticed the man brushing raindrops off the woman's cheeks with a gentle hand, and he looked away.

Brady saw that Holly was sitting in the back of the trolley with the microphone in her hand, but there were only a few passengers on the rainy day, and Holly gave them a half-hearted welcome and told them the next stop was in five minutes.

Bella swung her legs from the seat and hummed a song as she watched out the window. Brady sat back and rested an arm across the seat back so Bella wouldn't bump her head on the wood. Over the quiet trolley engine, Brady heard sirens behind them, getting closer. Kate pulled to the right and stopped the trolley, allowing the emergency vehicles passing room.

Brady got up and peered out the front windshield. The ladder truck, two pumpers, one rescue truck and an ambulance passed them. Kate glanced up. "Must be bad," she said.

Holly had also come to the front of the trolley to see what was going on. "Those trucks are flying," she commented.

"Maybe it's not as bad as it looks," Brady said. "Sometimes we empty out the station and we're back in fifteen minutes."

Brady heard more sirens and he clenched his jaw as he saw one of their older fire trucks speed past. It was usually a backup truck that only rolled on the most desperate occasions.

Bella got out of her seat and stood next to him, slipping her small hand into his. His phone beeped with a familiar tone that could only mean one thing. The station was calling in off-duty firefighters and volunteers. He pulled it from his pocket and confirmed the message. His heart sank and he swallowed hard. The fire was at a nursing home, and there were possible entrapped victims. That was as desperate as it got.

"Hate to ask this," he began, his voice deadly serious.

"What do you need?" Kate said. "Are you okay?"

Brady ran a hand over his face. "I need to go help, but I need a ride to the station and someone to take care of Bella until my brother comes to get her. I can't believe I'm asking…you don't have to do this. Maybe they'll get enough help with the volunteers… it's just that it's a bad—"

"Of course I'll help you." Kate swung her attention to Bella. "Would you mind being my partner while your uncle goes to rescue someone? I need someone to ring the bell at every stop."

Bella looked up at him, and her face almost broke his heart. She looked worried. "Will you be okay?" she asked.

"I sure will, honey," he said. "And my friend Kate will deliver you to your daddy as soon as he's finished talking to someone about a new job."

Bella smiled. "Okay."

Brady sat down and pulled Bella onto his lap. "You're going to have so much fun ringing that bell. I'm really jealous." Bella giggled and Brady held her close.

Kate did a U-turn in the street and headed in the direction of the fire station. She didn't blow the stop signs or speed, but she also didn't waste any time. Holly moved up and sat behind Brady. "I love kids," she said. "I'll help Kate keep an eye on Bella."

Brady turned and smiled at her. "Much appreciated."

"But I'm taking a picture and posting it on the app," Holly said.

What?

"I'm making your day, aren't I?" Holly explained.

Brady nodded congenially, but he was looking at Kate and knew she hadn't even thought of the game. She hadn't asked what the emergency was, just offered her help. Kate was a prize all by herself, no matter what happened with the employee app at the end of summer.

"I'm texting you my brother's number,"

Brady said as Kate drove. "Is it okay with you if I text him yours, Kate?"

"Yes." Kate rolled to a stop in front of the station and pulled the bell. She smiled. "All firefighters have to get off here," she called, trying to be cheerful, he could tell, for Bella's sake. "Watch your step."

Brady put Bella on the seat and kissed her hair, gave Kate's shoulder a quick squeeze on the way by and dashed down the trolley steps. All the doors to the fire station were open, most of the trucks gone. He saw volunteers suiting up as he ran for his locker. In his five years on the department, he'd been out on dozens of fire calls that came in as possible entrapments. He and his partners always hurried as fast as safety would allow, but knowing someone could be perishing behind a wall of flame had them pushing the trucks and punishing the sirens.

He jumped into the back seat of a truck that was already running, joining two volunteers and Charlie Zimmerman.

"About time you showed up," Charlie said with a quick grin. "Don't tell me you were home watching house-hunter shows on television."

"Babysitting my niece," Brady said. "Had to make a quick arrangement."

Charlie's expression sobered. "Hope the entrapment call was out of an abundance of caution and we find five dozen old folks under umbrellas in the front yard drinking coffee and watching us put out the fire."

Brady nodded. He finished snapping up his coat and worked his arms through the air pack mounted on the back of the seat. Charlie was doing the same thing, both of them planning to be ready to run as soon as the truck stopped at the fire scene. The rain fell in sheets, and the sky was dark even though it was midmorning.

The volunteer firefighter driving the truck sped through downtown Cape Pursuit, siren blaring. Brady looked out the side window and saw the Cape Pursuit trolley pulled over for them to pass. He couldn't see inside the trolley because of the rain, but he hoped Bella would be okay. Would his brother understand, or would he be angry that Brady had turned her over to someone else to go fight a fire?

The thought sent a twinge to his heart, but he had no doubt Kate would ensure Bella's safety and well-being. He tried not to think about the fact that Kate might want to step back from her tenuous summer romance with him because being tied down with a family was clearly not on her wish list. Asking her to babysit his niece would likely drive that point home.

As he saw a maze of flashing lights ahead and felt the truck slow down, he put thoughts of Kate and Bella out of his mind. He'd made his choice, and he had a job to do.

CHAPTER NINE

KATE ASKED HOLLY to drive so she could take the narrator's job and sit with Bella. She also made the executive decision to reroute the trolley so their path would not take them past the fire scene at what Kate discovered was a nursing home. No wonder Brady had seemed so serious. Any fire was sobering, but one at a facility housing senior citizens could be deadly. If something terrible had happened, she didn't want anyone on the trolley to be a witness.

"Your uncle is a hero," she told Bella. "Rushing off to save people."

"Uncle Brady," Bella said with a smile. "He's nice. He's letting us live at his house while my mommy tries to fix my grandpa."

Kate had wondered about Bella and Brady's brother. So they were all living together? Kate had never been to Brady's house, but she knew which street it was on and knew

A HOME FOR THE FIREFIGHTER

the houses on that street were mostly former cottages that were now rentals. Space had to be tight with two men and a little girl.

"I'm sorry your grandpa is broken," Kate said.

"He's at a hospital trying to get better."

"I hope he does."

Kate sat back, not knowing what to say to a four-year-old girl, and not feeling right about prying into Brady's family affairs. As open and honest as he was, he would probably tell her everything if she asked. Holly pulled up to a stop and Kate told Bella to stay seated while she helped people on and checked their tickets. Only two people boarded on the rainy day, and Kate hurried back to her seat with Brady's niece. No way did she want to disappoint him by shirking her responsibility as a babysitter. She loved her freedom, but she also tried never to let people down. Her parents… they were disappointed in her life's choices, but she hadn't made them any promises.

Kate had never been a babysitter as a teenager and, in fact, had never held a job at all until she left home right after graduation. Her parents were blessed financially, and they didn't want her to risk grease burns at a fast-food restaurant, get sunburned working as a lifeguard at the local pool, be required to work evenings and weekends in retail or have any part in the typical jobs available to teenagers. Although she was grateful for her perfectly kept home, her own room and parents who were always available, Kate had been anxious to leave home and get her hands dirty. She didn't want to be treated as a priceless object or a princess any longer, and she certainly never wanted to be married off at the country club as she'd seen happen to the other girls in her class.

Her parents never understood the jobs she took and the life she chose to lead. If they could see her babysitting a coworker's niece on a trolley in the rain right now, they would think she needed pot roast, new shoes and a peaceful evening at home.

Her phone chimed and she looked at the message.

Is this Kate Price? the message said.

Yes, is this Noah?

Kate was glad they had briefly met before, so she would recognize him. There was no way she was handing Bella over to a stranger. She arranged a meeting place two trolley stops away via text message and told Bella her dad would meet them soon. The little girl smiled as if it was a great adventure. She seemed to have the same sunny attitude as Brady and take things in stride. Was it a family trait? Kate's own parents considered a deviation from the expected to be just that— a deviation, which was bad.

"Thank you," Noah said when he stepped on board the trolley and his daughter rushed him for a hug. "You're a real hero, just like my brother. You two are definitely made for each other."

Kate had no idea what Brady had told his brother about their relationship, but his words caused a balloon of nervousness to expand in her chest. *Made for each other.* Kate was operating on the philosophy that she was made for herself and the life of adventure she had planned.

"Just trying to help," she said.

Late that afternoon, Kate was back in her small apartment. Holly had gone out with a friend for dinner, but Kate had put up her hair, pulled on sweatpants and a cozy sweater and put on her reading glasses. She had a paperback novel about a woman who followed her dream and became a tour guide, traveling all over Europe, meeting new people, seeing castles and waterways, churches and mountains.

Before she opened her book, she checked the employee app on her phone. She wasn't scheduled to work the next two days because she had traded some shifts to grab some time off for a short trip. She hadn't mentioned the trip to Brady because she wasn't sure she could get the two days she needed, and she wasn't sure now how to say it. He wasn't exactly her boyfriend and she didn't owe him an explanation of her time. And she probably wouldn't see him, anyway, before she left early in the morning. There would be time to tell him about it when she got back.

She heard the hallway door outside her apartment slam. It often did that when it was windy and whoever was entering wasn't familiar with the door's quirks. She listened. It was a heavy footstep, not Holly's, and then she heard a knock on her door. Kate peeked through the hole. If she didn't know Brady, she might not have opened the door. His hair was sticking up all over, his face was streaked with dirt and his shirt looked as if he'd worn it for a week.

She opened the door. "Are you okay?"

He attempted a smile. "Filthy and I smell like a three-day campfire, but I'm fine."

He certainly was fine. Brady was heroic, attractive, funny and sincere. Most women would be tossing a rope around him and dragging him into their apartments. "Were the people at the fire all right?" Kate asked. "We drove by and I saw it was the nursing home, but then I rerouted the trolley to stay out of the way and so Bella wouldn't see."

"Thank you. You were a real lifesaver."

Kate swung the door open wide and waved for him to come in. "Says the man who actually saves lives all the time."

"Not today," he said.

"Oh, no, did someone—"

"No, I mean we didn't have to save them. The staff at that care facility did a great job getting everyone out. The initial report said they were missing someone, but it turned out he was in the bathroom." Brady gave a tired smile. "They're all okay, but it's going to be a long rest of the day as they find new places for the residents to stay. Only one wing of the place is seriously damaged, but there's smoke and water throughout. It's no place for someone to live right now."

Kate smelled smoke and sweat and dampness on him, but she didn't mind. What bothered her was the exhaustion in the lines of Brady's face and a thin red cut across his cheekbone. She reached up and touched his cheek just below the cut. "What happened?"

"Stupidity," he said. "I was pulling down a section of ceiling when the fire was mostly out, and a piece of metal got me. It's minor."

Kate closed the door and pointed to two stools in her small kitchen. "I could heat up some soup or make you a grilled cheese sandwich," she offered. "Coffee?"

Brady shook his head, and he didn't sit down. "We had pizza at the station that someone sent us. People are nice like that, and food seems to come out of nowhere just when we really need it. I'm on my way home to shower, but I had to stop and see you first." He took her hand in his large rough one, but his touch was gentle. "There aren't many people I'd trust with my niece, even some people I've known for a long time. But I never had a doubt about her safety leaving her with you. There's something special about you, Kate."

Kate didn't speak, but she put her free hand on his shoulder and waited. He was the special one, and he deserved someone who would be around to appreciate it.

"I want to hold you close, even though I know I have to let you go at the end of the summer," Brady said. He leaned in and put a soft kiss on her forehead. Kate tilted her head and her lips found his as she closed her eyes and let herself enjoy the sensation. She'd never met anyone like Brady, never been so tempted to settle in for the night with a good man who wanted nothing more than to be there the next day and the next.

"I have to go," Brady said.

Kate wanted to ask why, but she knew it was wiser to say good night. She kissed him once more, and he smiled at her and left. She went to the window and watched him head toward his truck. He moved like a man who was physically exhausted, but the rain had stopped and a streak of sun lit up his hair as he climbed in.

She wished he would have stayed for a cup

of coffee, and her apartment seemed lonely and empty after he left. Kate tried to ignore the faint smoky smell he left behind as she grabbed her small overnight bag and started packing. Before she went to bed that night, she had her clothes picked out and her route planned.

The next morning, Kate went out to the parking lot before the sun came up and put her purse and one piece of luggage in the back seat of her two-year-old Ford Escape. Both the name of the car and its size had appealed to her when she bought the car new. Kate had saved her money and paid cash because, without a permanent address or much credit history to speak of, she wasn't a good candidate for a car loan. Her parents would have helped her out and insisted she buy a more expensive car, but she wasn't going to ask them. She would have been just as happy buying a cheap used vehicle, but she drove for Uber whenever she stayed in a place long enough to learn the geography, and for that she needed a nice car. The money in chauffeuring people around was decent, but she usually only drove when she really needed the cash. When she returned from her trip to

Florida, she planned to take up Uber driving in Cape Pursuit for the rest of the summer— if her trip went well and her dream of being a flight attendant became reality.

Kate got on the highway and headed south. The Daytona airport was a twelve-hour drive, and she had a hotel room near the airport reserved. Her appointment with the admissions office at the flight attendant school was early the next morning, and if all went as planned, she would be back on the road by noon and back to Cape Pursuit by midnight tomorrow. She'd told Holly she was going to Florida to check out a school, but Holly had been engaged in a lengthy text conversation with some man she met on the beach, and Kate suspected her roommate had hardly heard a word she said.

It didn't matter. Kate was used to being on her own and not having anyone checking on her or waiting up for her. The twelve-hour drive stretched before her like a delicious plate of appetizers. The road signs, freeway on-ramps and mile markers invited and urged her on, and she relished hitting the cruise control and seeing the trees and buildings fly past. She stopped twice for gas and once for food, and she checked into her airport hotel before sunset.

The next day, Kate put on a nice dark-blue skirt and a crisp white blouse, the kind of thing she'd seen flight attendants wear. She put up her hair, slipped into low heels and even tied a jaunty scarf around her neck before she marched into the recruiting office. Her tour included training areas for flight attendants, classroom facilities and mock-ups of airplanes simulating the job environment. Kate felt right at home in an occupation that was all about getting away, and when she sat down with the admissions representative, she completed the paperwork with excitement blossoming in her heart.

When the admissions representative offered her financial aid applications and suggested a scholarship might be available, Kate turned it down at first. She wanted to do this on her own, and with the cash saved up from her previous job and the extra hours she was putting in during the summer, she'd be able to do it. Had to do it. However, the admissions representative had insisted and told her that at least a one-thousand-dollar scholarship was standard, offered to everyone by a corporate sponsor, and she'd only be cheating herself if she didn't fill out the brief application.

In the car on the way home, Kate listened to the lengthy playlist of music she'd put together two years earlier as she crossed the continent while working for the freight line. She called the playlist "road music," and it usually made her feel as if she could drive forever. However, driving north toward Cape Pursuit felt…different. She didn't usually look forward to the destination as much as the journey, but she wanted to tell someone—Holly, George…Brady—about her enrollment in flight attendant school and have someone to share her excitement with.

She couldn't call Brady. He would probably be at work at the fire station or even on the trolley.

Kate decided to call her parents instead. It had been easily a month since she'd heard their voices, even though she did text with them every few days to check in and say hello. She loved them, and she knew they loved her even if they would never understand her choices and they asked her to come home every chance they could.

Her mother answered on the third ring and she sounded slightly breathless.

"So sorry, honey, I was vacuuming so I'd have everything clean when your father gets home," her mother said.

Kate rolled her eyes and nearly joined her mother on the last five words. How many times had she heard those words?

"That's okay, Mom, I'm just calling to say hello and tell you my great news."

"You're coming home!"

"I'm not coming home, but I am enrolling in school," Kate said.

"Not truck driving school again. Your father and I just hate thinking of you all alone out there on the road somewhere where there could be maniacs and murderers."

"I never saw any up close, but I'm sure there are probably maniacs and murderers not too far from your house, Mom," Kate said. She regretted her words as soon as she said them, imagining her mother having additional security cameras or alarms installed on her home, which was already safer than a bank.

To cover the silence from the other end, Kate told her mother all about flight attendant school, the training and the job prospects and how she'd finally found her calling in life.

"Is that safe?" her mother asked.

"Sure it is," Kate said. "Flying is statistically safer than driving."

"What are you doing right now?"

"Driving from Daytona back to Cape Pursuit. I only have about nine hours to go."

More silence on the other end.

Kate sighed. "I just wanted to share my good news, and tell you I love you and Dad and hope you're doing well."

Her mother assured her she loved her and said she would pass on everything Kate had said as soon as her father got home. Kate had no doubt she would.

Feeling as if the wings of her excitement had been clipped or coated with concrete, Kate tried to cheer herself up by putting her road music playlist back on, but it didn't have the effect she wanted. It would be too late to call Brady when she got home or ask him to meet her for a late-night drink. He wanted to be a homebody so desperately he was looking at houses with a Realtor, but Kate still thought he understood her desire for freedom and accepted her feelings as valid. It was nice, and she thought of Brady's warm eyes and smile for the next one hundred miles.

CHAPTER TEN

"Preapproval," Charlie told Brady as they waited for the state fire inspector to show up at the scene of the previous day's nursing home fire. "The trick to buying the home you want is to know for sure how much the bank is willing to bet on you."

"I'm almost afraid to guess," Brady said.

Charlie ducked beneath a piece of yellow caution tape and held it up for Brady to step under. "You could probably get an appointment later today or sometime tomorrow and sit down with a loan officer. I think you're going to be pleasantly surprised. I've gotten people into really nice houses who weren't half as good a risk as you."

"I have no collateral and not enough down payment," Brady argued. He hated getting his hopes up, even though he knew Charlie had expertise in this realm. Would his friend mislead him? No. But Charlie also had no idea that Brady had started life with absolutely nothing and was very slowly building.

Charlie shrugged. "The house itself is the collateral. That's how it works. You pay on it your whole life, and then you retire debt free, die and leave it to your kids. It's the American dream."

Brady laughed. "Is that how it worked for you?"

"Nope. My dad is still enjoying his house, and Jane and I are making mortgage payments just like everyone else." Charlie cocked his head and gave Brady a long look. "You never mention your parents."

Brady pulled off a chunk of siding that was hanging down in front of the facility's entrance. It came loose with a loud groan and Brady tossed it into a pile of debris in the front yard. His heart ached for the infirm and elderly residents who had spent the night somewhere else after being suddenly uprooted. He knew what that felt like, the fear and uncertainty. He'd experienced it as a child, but he imagined the feelings were much the same for anyone, regardless of age.

"Nothing to brag about," Brady said. Charlie meant well, and there was no reason to keep his childhood a secret. "Never met my dad, wouldn't know him if I saw him. I'd like to think my mom was doing the best she could as a single parent, but, man, it didn't really look that way to Noah and me. We slept in a lot of different places when we were kids."

Charlie crossed his arms and leaned against the front wall of the fire-ravaged building. "You don't have to live like that anymore. Or your brother. You'll never be rich doing this job, but if you'll take my advice and go see that loan officer, I think you could be putting up Christmas lights on your own house this December."

Brady smiled. "I've never done that."

"If you get good at it, you can come over to my place and put them up. To Jane's satisfaction, of course. She has an artist's eye, and I think my efforts last Christmas were not quite what she had in mind." Charlie laughed. "She said it looked like a cartoon character had tried to hang outdoor decorations. I don't think it was a compliment."

Brady let himself dream about putting up outdoor lights and an artificial tree in his own spacious living room. As a firefighter, he wouldn't have a fresh-cut evergreen in his home, too much of a hazard. But he'd buy the best-looking artificial tree and have his brother and niece help him decorate it. They would put out cookies and milk for Santa. He'd drink coffee with Noah while Bella opened presents under the tree on Christmas morning. Seeing Kate over a cup of steaming coffee would complete the fantasy, but he knew that was as likely as flying reindeer landing on the beach at Cape Pursuit.

He shook off the thoughts that were so real to him he could almost smell the cookies and coffee. It was too tempting, too indulgent to even hope for. Brady glanced up and saw the state fire inspector's truck at the curb, and it was both a disappointment and a relief to get his thoughts back on work.

"This guy's going to have a lot of questions," Charlie said. "The chief owes us one for meeting the state inspector here and babysitting him while he walks through."

"Chief still has to do the paperwork," Brady said. "I think we're getting the easy job."

Two hours later, Charlie and Brady got back in the fire department pickup truck, and

Charlie drove toward the station. He held out his phone to Brady as he kept one hand on the wheel. "Scroll through my contacts and you'll find two banks in Cape Pursuit I think give people a fair shake. Call and make an appointment."

Brady took the phone and tapped the screen to bring it to life. "I don't know," he said.

"Trust me. Any chance your brother can contribute to the buying effort? I'm assuming he's going to keep living with you, but I don't know what his deal is."

Brady blew out a breath. "I'm not sure what his long-range plan is, either. His girlfriend has a family illness issue this summer, and she's trusting him with Bella. I'm trying to make sure he does such a great job that he gets at least shared custody. I like having them in my house and feeling like a family."

"What does Kate think of that?"

Brady paused in his scrolling when he found the first bank in Charlie's contact list. It was the one where his brother applied for the accounting job. Should he skip that one? He had no idea if his brother would be offered a job there, and if he was, would it be a conflict of interest to apply for a loan? Better go with the other one, he thought as he found the other bank and transferred the phone number into his own contact list.

"So I'm getting ignored on the whole Kate question," Charlie said. "Okay."

"I was copying the phone number for the bank so I could take your pushy advice," Brady said, grinning at his friend. "And I have no idea what to say about Kate except that I'm sure I'll be saying goodbye to her again in September, probably for good."

"Scaring her away two years in a row, huh?"

Brady tucked his phone in his shirt pocket and leaned back in the seat. "She's not the kind of person who scares easily, but she's got a whole plan for her life that doesn't include settling down here or anywhere."

"Good for her, I guess," Charlie said. "I gave up making plans when I found out Jane was expecting our daughter. Right now, I'm just trying to survive diapers and teething."

"You're loving every minute of it," Brady said.

"You're not wrong," Charlie said as he pulled into the fire station and cut the engine.

After a minor ambulance call and a late

lunch, Brady called the loan department at the bank and, to his surprise, got a late-afternoon appointment. His gut twisted with nervousness at the thought of sitting across from someone and exposing his financial fitness for home ownership. Would they laugh at him and tell him he was several years away from even thinking about it? He'd tried researching loans online, but always ended up giving up out of exasperation and…fear. What did he know about being a home owner and settling down? He'd never had a dad who showed him how to put up a ladder and clean out the gutters. He'd never even mowed a lawn until he got a job as a firefighter in Cape Pursuit and rented the house he was still living in. His mother had never needed him or Noah to install a dishwasher or repair a window because she had never owned a house or stayed in one place very long.

Maybe he wasn't qualified to own a house… maybe wanting it wasn't enough?

He would find out. There was no way to back out, not with Charlie encouraging him and asking pointed questions. And he owed it to Noah and Bella to put on a brave face and lay out his tax returns, pay stubs and banking information to be judged by someone across a desk at the bank.

With over an hour to spare between work and his appointment, Brady planned to stop by home and grab the paperwork he kept in a small fire-safe box. He decided to wear his firefighter's uniform of a navy-blue shirt with the Cape Pursuit Fire Department symbol over the chest pocket. He would look professional and employed when he went to the bank, and that couldn't hurt. Brady pulled up the employee app on his phone, wondering if Kate was on the schedule or if she might be at her place. He scrolled through the roster. No Kate.

Seeing her for even a few minutes would be nice. He still needed to find a way to thank her for taking care of Bella, and showing up at her house not smelling like a fire would be a step in the right direction. Maybe he could ask her to dinner after his bank meeting.

Brady pulled his truck into Kate's apartment parking lot and got out, feeling buoyant. She wouldn't be impressed by his excitement over a home loan, but he wanted to tell someone about it. He didn't see her car in the parking lot, but he knocked on her door anyway, hoping. There were voices inside, he noted happily, but when Holly opened the door, Brady felt a slice of disappointment.

"She's gone," Holly said without any preamble. "Took off early this morning, I think."

"Gone?" The word left a hollow feeling in Brady's chest.

Holly wasn't alone in the apartment. A man lounged on the secondhand couch in the living room. In answer to his question, Holly shrugged. "I'm not in charge of her schedule, and I can't remember what she told me when she was talking about leaving."

Brady's stomach sank and he wished he hadn't made the impulsive decision to stop by and see Kate. He'd been a fool to think Kate would be waiting at home for him to share his feelings about the bank visit. She had her own life, own plans, and he was well aware that they didn't include him no matter how much he wished they could.

"Do you know when she'll be back?" Brady asked. The way Holly said *gone* made it sound final. He wanted to ask Holly *if* Kate would be back, but Holly was preoccupied with her company and didn't seem to have any knowledge she was willing to share.

It had been just like this last September. A kiss on the beach one evening, and then Kate was gone the next day, forever as far as Brady knew at the time. She wouldn't just disappear again, would she? And long before the summer ended? Had he done something to drive her away, no matter how careful he'd been to respect her space?

"Did she take everything with her?" he asked.

"She doesn't have much," Holly said. "Sorry," she added, her eyes straying to her guest as if she wanted Brady to go away.

"Thanks, anyway," Brady said. "Sorry to bother you." He went out to his truck and got in, but he didn't start it. He rested his forehead on the top of the steering wheel, hoping maybe Kate would pull in if he just waited a few minutes. Time ticked by, and he knew he had to get going to his appointment or risk being late. He considered calling or texting Kate. Would it hurt to tell her he was thinking of her? Was she thinking about him when she left early that morning without leaving any kind of a message for him? Had she really taken everything with her? He wished he had taken a closer inventory of the apartment the one other time he'd been in it... Did it seem empty now?

He sighed, started the truck and drove to the bank parking lot. He called his brother's cell phone. Noah had not been home during Brady's brief stop to pick up his paperwork, but Brady needed to hear a friendly voice, someone who was always on his side.

"Are you busy?" Brady asked. It was unreasonable to hope that Noah would be able to go with him to the bank appointment. There was Bella to consider, and Noah didn't really have anything to contribute. But still, he wanted his brother's support.

"I'm walking home from the library with Bella. She checked out about fifteen books that all look the same to me. Bedtime is going to go on forever tonight."

Brady smiled, thinking about how nice it would be to help tuck in his niece and offer to read a story or two. He remembered his mother reading a book to him and Noah a few times when they were little. There wasn't always a room of their own or even a bed, but their mother had tried, sometimes.

"Did you need something?" Noah asked.

"No," Brady said. He wanted to ask for

Noah's help or encouragement, but his brother had enough going on, his own responsibilities. Brady would do what he could to provide a permanent home without burdening his brother or pressuring him to contribute in any way. Brady was the older sibling, and he had always tried to shelter Noah. "Just wanted to say hello. I'll be home around six. Want me to pick up dinner?"

"That would be great. Try to get something with vegetables if you can so I don't feel like a bad father."

Brady laughed. "I'll get the kids' meal with the carrots and applesauce so you won't have to feel guilty."

As he gathered up his tax returns and pay stubs, Brady told himself to toughen up. He hadn't had a father to teach him about home maintenance, but Noah had a bigger problem. He hadn't had a father to teach him how to be a dad, and yet he was giving it everything he had every day. Brady could face a loan officer if his younger brother could face the responsibility of taking care of another human being.

CHAPTER ELEVEN

BRADY HATED BEING glad about a busy day at the station because being on the run meant other people were having a lousy day. Two car accidents, one medical emergency at a beach hotel and a potentially disastrous house fire were miserable for the people involved, even though it was good for Brady to have barely a moment to sit down, eat or think about Kate.

Saving someone's home from destruction had come at the right moment for him, just when he was questioning his passion for owning his own home. Not that the meeting at the bank had gone badly, but Brady had had a hard time interpreting the poker face of the loan officer who told him they would get back to him in seven to ten days with a preliminary loan amount he could qualify for.

The other thing he needed was communication from Kate, even if it came in the form of closure. He was scheduled for the morning shift on the trolley after two long days of hearing and seeing nothing of Kate. He'd looked on the employee app, of course. Kate was also scheduled for the day shift. Would she show up? He couldn't imagine her leaving George and the company high and dry, but the one thing he knew about her was her rock-solid plan for not sticking around.

"Hello," Kate said, looking up and smiling as soon as Brady entered the break room at the trolley office and held up his card to swipe it through the time clock. His first thought was that she was there, still in Cape Pursuit. His second thought was that she looked radiant and happy. His third thought involved kissing her, but it came so closely on the heels of his other impressions that he could hardly tell his emotions apart.

"Hi," he said, unsure what to say next. For him, so much had happened since he'd seen her, but what had been going on with her? She deserved the chance to tell him, and they had at least ten minutes before the first trolley was scheduled to depart. "I missed you."

"I was gone less than two days," she said. She used the break room coffeepot to refill her travel mug, and she didn't look at him.

"Hardly enough to even notice," she added in a low voice.

"I noticed." He wanted to add that it would have been nice if she'd mentioned she was going to be gone and when she would be back—that she would even be back. But he didn't. Did a summer romance involve such terms? Did he have to check in with her if he was going to be out late?

"I didn't want to bother you because I know you work a lot," she said. Her voice faltered a bit. "So I didn't call or text."

"I wouldn't have minded." Brady slid his employee identification card back into his wallet. He separated a disposable coffee cup from the stack, and Kate took it and filled it for him. She put it on the counter next to the creamer and sugar, but she didn't touch him even though she stood very close to him.

"You didn't call or text me, either," Kate said.

Brady nodded. There was no refuting the point. "Holly said you'd gone away."

"On a short trip."

"She didn't say that. She didn't seem to know or be willing to share any details when

I stopped by your house the day before yesterday."

"You came by?" Kate's expression softened and she leaned one hip on the counter and faced him. Her eyes were inviting, but Brady had too many questions.

"I wanted to tell you…well, I just wanted to thank you again for helping me and Noah with Bella."

Kate's brow wrinkled and she looked down. "You already said thank you."

Why did she seem disappointed? Was she hoping he had another reason for coming to her place?

"You don't have to tell me where you went," he said. "I know we agreed to a short-term, no-strings summer…thing. But I'll tell you what I did for the last two days because you've probably noticed I'm an open book."

"Are you?" she asked.

Brady was surprised by her tone that almost implied a challenge. He'd been nothing but honest with her, and he had to be honest with himself in acknowledging that opening his heart to a flight risk like Kate was going to lead to misery sooner or later.

"I helped clean up after the nursing home

fire, went to the bank for preapproval on a house loan, read five books to Bella before she finally fell asleep, worked at the station, put out a house fire and…still had time to miss you."

Kate smiled and put a hand on his shoulder. "You've been busy."

"And you?"

"I drove to Daytona and met with the flight attendant school's admissions office."

"Long drive," Brady commented. "Now it makes sense."

"I told Holly where I was going, but I had the impression she wasn't listening."

"Next time you should tell someone who's paying attention," Brady said.

Like me.

Kate's smile faded and she dropped her hand from his shoulder, and Brady had the distinct feeling he'd overstepped. He didn't want Kate to think he was checking up on her or didn't trust her to take care of herself, but he—literally—lived to keep people safe. It wasn't only his job. He'd seen the hard knocks of the world all his life, and he couldn't let someone he cared about put herself in danger. He considered it a miracle that his mother hadn't fallen victim to violence with the life she had led.

"I'd love to hear about your trip," Brady said, mustering enthusiasm. "How about over dinner tonight?"

Kate hesitated and bit her lip, and Brady could see a *no* coming. "I'm not free tonight," Kate said. "I'm driving for Uber."

He tried very hard not to react. Not to raise an eyebrow, draw in a sharp breath or tighten his jaw. Considering the big step Kate took as she shoved away from the break room counter, he knew he hadn't been successful. Her stories of driving for a truck line, crossing the lonely roads of the United States alone...those were in the past and he knew she'd survived. However, putting herself in the risky position of driving strangers around, that made the muscles on the back of his neck tighten.

"It's a good way to earn extra cash," Kate said. "You should consider it."

"I don't think anyone would want to ride in my eight-year-old truck," he said. He tried to lighten his tone. He really didn't have a right to judge what Kate did in her spare time, and she was clearly more than capable of handling herself. She'd be on jets flying all over the world soon, making driving tourists around a beach town seem tame by comparison. He smiled, trying to remember that his summer romance with Kate was about taking advantage of the short time and thin slice of happiness she was offering. "My truck smells like the fire station even though I put one of those air freshener things in it when my brother brought my niece to stay."

"Does it smell like fake flowers and candles now?" Kate asked, her shoulders relaxing and her smile returning.

"I got the mountain pine scent, but I have no idea how accurate it is. You've smelled mountain pines, I'm guessing, with all your hiking all over the country. Maybe you can be the judge next time you're in my truck."

"Something to look forward to," she said.

Brady leaned against the counter and Kate edged closer. "Which is one more reason why you should skip driving for Uber tonight and have a dinner date with me instead."

Not to mention she'd be far safer in his company. She cocked her head and gave him a long assessing look, and Brady was afraid she was going to announce an early departure for flight attendant school or an abrupt end to their summer…relationship. To his surprise, she glanced around the break room and then closed the distance between them to put a hand on his cheek and her lips on his. She gave him a long kiss that seemed to be full of promises of warm summer nights under the stars.

"Rain check on the dinner," she said, and she turned to go out to the trolleys and start her workday.

Maybe summer romance was a better name for whatever was between them, after all.

KATE GREETED HER passengers and clicked the confirm button on her app. She loaded the address of their destination into her phone so her passengers could see it, even though she knew almost every street in Cape Pursuit by heart. The couple in the back seat of her red Escape told her they were on their honeymoon, just a short trip because neither one of them could afford to take much time off work. They chatted about the wonderful trips they hoped to take—someday—on their short drive from their hotel to a widely known seafood restaurant on the other end of town. Kate suggested several national parks they might like if they ever got to take a longer trip, and she was pleased to see they left her a generous tip after she dropped them off.

Kate circled around to the beach area where she parked for five minutes before her app notified her of another pickup. Her next three sets of passengers were all friendly tourists enjoying a night out. A lull set in, and Kate parked on a downtown street, waiting for a request. Ten minutes went by, and she became restless sitting behind the wheel. What was Brady doing since she'd turned him down for a dinner date? A nice guy like him probably didn't lack for friends to go out with. Or was he at home enjoying the security of four walls that seemed so important to him?

Kate turned down a side street that led to an intersection with a larger street running parallel to the tourist district. She knew Brady lived on the northern edge of the desirable rental neighborhoods. He'd told her as much himself, and then she couldn't help noticing his address in the company paperwork she was currently in charge of. It wasn't really snooping. Brady would tell her his exact address and probably social security number if she asked.

She drove slowly down his street, glancing at addresses on the homes that were all similar. They were previously vacation cottages, but current owners had expanded them with porches, additions and even a second story in some cases. She saw Brady's gray pickup sitting in the driveway of a house and she didn't have to look at the numbers anymore.

His house was already small, and the double driveway, front doors and mailboxes made it clear that it was a duplex. He shared half a small house with his brother and niece? He was even nicer than she'd realized. She'd had her own bedroom, bathroom and walk-in closet as a child. Brady's half-a-house would almost fit into the space where Kate had enjoyed growing up.

Lights were on in the front window and the garage door was up as Kate cruised slowly by. The light was also on in the garage, and she could clearly see Brady working on something. Was it a bicycle? Kate slowed down to get a better look just as Brady glanced up and saw her.

She couldn't keep driving. He'd caught her spying on him. Brady straightened up from his project and came out of the garage, waving at her. Kate sighed, backed up and pulled into his driveway. As soon as she rolled down her window, Brady leaned in. He glanced into the back seat.

"No passengers?"

"Not right now. It's been pretty busy up until the last twenty minutes."

"Bar-hoppers?" he asked.

Kate shook her head. "Honeymooners and some tourists. Some of them were going to bars, so I imagine I might see them again at the end of the night."

"Want me to ride along with you as your bodyguard?"

"I don't need a bodyguard."

"Then I could give a narrated tour, local color, like on the trolley."

Kate laughed. "People who call for a ride aren't looking for entertainment. They want to get from point A to point B as quickly and cheaply as they can." She nodded toward the garage. "What are you working on?"

"Training wheels on my niece's bicycle. We went shopping after dinner and found a bike just the right size for her, but she needs the training wheels unless we want to run alongside her and hold up the bicycle."

"That would be tiring."

"I can tell you from only a five-minute ex-perience that it's brutal. I'd rather haul a fire hose up a ladder," Brady said.

Kate's phone beeped with a notification of a ride request, and she took the phone from the holder and acknowledged the call.

"I have to go," she said.

Brady nodded. "Will I see you tomorrow?"

"The scavenger hunt kickoff is bright and early," she said. "I helped George with some of the planning, but he was going to use a computer program to randomly match play-ers early tomorrow morning after he gives people one more night to sign up. You signed up, didn't you?"

Kate had only signed up because of loyalty to her boss and her temporary position as his helper. When she had first seen the activity posted, it had seemed as if it was too great a time investment, even though the participa-tion points and the bonus for winning were highly motivating.

"I'll sign up if you are," Brady said.

"There's no guarantee we'll be teamed up together."

"Then we'll have to compare notes over dinner."

He leaned in the car window and kissed her, and the sweetness of his kiss and his nearness made her wish she could stay. Kate pulled back and put her car in Reverse, reminding herself that she had a job and a goal. Brady's face showed disappointment, but he didn't say anything. She backed out of the driveway and waved as she headed downtown for her pickup. She couldn't ask her riders to wait another minute, even though it had been hard tearing herself away from Brady.

When darkness fell, she picked up two men and then two women who'd had too much to drink, but aside from being sloppy in their directions, they were harmless. People didn't scare Kate nearly as much as being tied down and making choices for her life out of fear and a desire for safety. Behind the wheel, she was in control and that control empowered her.

If Brady could see that Uber driving is perfectly safe and nice, he'd take back his offer of being her bodyguard. It had been tempting to trade an evening of work for an evening with Brady. Would he have given her a tour of his house? What was it like to be inside his world? She still wanted to tell him all about her visit to the school and share her excitement, but she was afraid he wouldn't understand her passion for getting away. Not a guy whose passion required him to keep both feet on the ground.

Kate signed out of her driving app after midnight, more than a hundred dollars richer but also knowing that morning would come early and she'd have to be focused on the launch of the employee scavenger hunt. Whoever she got paired up with for the twenty-four-hour time limit for completing the activity, he or she would have to be flexible if Kate got called in to work an extra shift on the trolley or an afternoon in the boss's office. She couldn't pass up an opportunity to grow her bank account because she only had a limited amount of time, and summer was already going fast. Every fleeting moment took her closer to her dream job…and closer to saying goodbye to Cape Pursuit—and Brady.

CHAPTER TWELVE

BRADY FINISHED UP his niece's bicycle and took advantage of a few minutes of daylight to watch her try it out in the driveway before bedtime. She crashed into the side of his truck once, but he rubbed out the scratch with his palm and told her it added to the truck's personality. Bella appeared on the point of tears, but she'd laughed when he licked his finger, rubbed it on the scratch and declared it all better. It had been a beautiful evening, especially when Kate had pulled into his driveway and he'd said good night with a kiss.

Before he turned in for the night, he logged into his phone and signed up for the scavenger hunt because Kate wanted him to. If he was the luckiest guy in Cape Pursuit, he'd get paired up with her, but there were probably at least twenty employees signing up. The odds were more likely he'd be scouring the town for strange items with someone he didn't know and like as much as he did Kate. The sign-up officially ended at midnight, and the matchups were supposed to be posted by seven the next morning. He'd have to take his chances.

Brady woke up, showered early and grabbed his phone just after seven to see if the teams were announced. His shoulders sank when he saw his partner. He loved the thrill of the hunt, but he'd been randomly matched with someone who didn't impress him much with her responsibility or work ethic. Holly. He'd hoped for Kate and got her roommate instead. Still, he couldn't let Holly—or anyone—down, so he showed up five minutes early and waited outside the door of the beach office for the official rules and the list of items they'd have a full day to find. It was a beautiful summer day. How bad could it be?

"Hey," Kate said, giving him a sympathetic look. "I already told Holly she couldn't lose interest or wander off on you. You deserve a shot at winning."

"Who's your partner?" Brady asked.

Kate leaned close and whispered, "Tom the Summer Heartbreaker."

Brady tilted his head back and stared at the sky. "Not ideal."

"I'd try to trade him, but I don't want to offend him," Kate said.

Brady felt a glimmer of satisfaction and hope. "Are you saying you'd rather be teamed up with me?"

"Of course I would," she said. "It's a scavenger hunt, and a local like you with in-depth knowledge has a much better chance of winning. You probably know everyone in town, and they'll be motivated to help you because you're a firefighter."

"And a nice guy," he added.

Kate laughed. "And a nice guy."

"So, about that trade."

"Shh," she said, one finger over her beautiful lips. Brady wanted to kiss that finger and her lips, but they were in a group of at least two dozen people in the bright morning light.

"Who'd you get?" Holly asked, running up breathlessly with less than one minute to spare. She grabbed Kate's phone and looked at it without waiting for a response. Her expression changed to joy and excitement. "We're trading," she said.

"What?" Kate asked.

Brady hoped Kate wouldn't argue because he would happily trade Holly for Kate.

"I've been trying to convince Tom to take a chance on a nice girl like me," Holly said. "But he's had his eyes on just about everyone else."

Not exactly a recommendation, Brady thought. Maybe Kate was right about being concerned for Holly's well-being.

"So you give me Tom and you can have whoever I got stuck with," Holly said. She handed Kate her phone, and Brady nearly laughed out loud at Kate's expression. It was partly disapproval of her friend's rudeness, but he saw satisfaction there, too. *Kate would rather be with me.* Maybe this scavenger hunt was going to go his way, after all.

"I believe you were stuck with Brady," Kate said. "But I'm willing to be saddled with a local hero so you can work on your love life. I'd do that for you."

"Thanks," Holly said, her eyes scanning the crowd. She didn't even appear to recognize Kate's sarcasm.

Brady couldn't resist slipping an arm around Kate's shoulders as Holly found Tom the Summer Heartbreaker in the crowd and scurried over to him. The dozens of summer employees waiting outside the office were all people Brady recognized, some of them locals making extra cash, and some of them returning summer workers from the previous year. He liked and respected most of them, but Kate was different. Being with her felt like warm summer rain and sparkling sunshine all mixed together.

"We're going to be a great team," he said, his voice low with excitement at his newfound good luck. His sense of self-preservation had served him well throughout a difficult childhood and during tense and dangerous situations as a firefighter. However, he chose to ignore the voice in his head reminding him not to get in too deep with someone who would break his heart. Spending the day with Kate was too hard to resist.

Kate smiled up at him. "I have high hopes."

"Rules," George said, holding up sheets of paper. The gathered workers grew silent. "You can go in any order you want, but you have to be back here by eight o'clock tomorrow morning, and you can't call off work if you're scheduled. It's an automatic disqualification, sorry to say."

"Can't believe how lucky we are," Kate

said. "We both work a short shift this afternoon, but we'll still have plenty of time."

Brady knew she was talking about time to find the required items for the scavenger hunt, but he felt as if he'd never have enough time with her. She wore a bright yellow T-shirt that contrasted with her dark hair and blue eyes, and the smile she gave him was worth a thousand sunrises.

"I hope you don't get called into the fire station," she said. "I'm looking forward to having fun with you." She nodded toward their boss, who was handing out papers, one to each team. "And winning, of course."

"I'll do my best," Brady said, but he didn't know if Kate heard him as she stepped forward and grabbed one of the rule and list sheets.

She smiled at him and held up the paper. "Here we go. This says we can use any form of transportation we want, but we have to stay together as a team and prove we were together at each location with pictures."

"I'll drive," he said. Without a word, he and Kate dashed toward his gray pickup and hopped in.

"Mermaid statue," she said. "First stop."

KATE TOOK A deep breath as she put on her seat belt. "I've never been in the fire station, so I can't tell you if it smells like that in here, but I'm not smelling a mountain pine, either."

"That's what I was afraid of," Brady said.

"Do you park inside the fire station?"

"No, but it lingers on me. Smoke, trucks, tires." He smiled. "It's a good smell."

"Then you shouldn't try to cover it up. I don't mind truck smell," Kate said. "I enjoyed most of my time driving across the country in one."

"You didn't get lonely? I'd lose my mind with only myself to talk to all day long."

Kate laughed. "I listened to audiobooks, called my parents every few days and talked to waiters at restaurants. It wasn't so bad."

The hours of solitude in the cab of her freight truck weren't the thing she remembered most. She could pull up detailed mental images of the road ahead, the mountains, the fields, even the cities she'd driven through. In just a few months, she could be experiencing the same freedom from the air.

Kate concentrated on the list of items they needed to find in Cape Pursuit. The list was long and daunting, and even though they weren't required to collect every single item, they would receive points for each thing they checked off. "Place mat from the Seafood Shack, that's an easy one," she said. "One plastic sandwich bag filled with beach sand. Three pieces of beach glass. A used Frisbee. One half of a bikini—your choice which half. One pair of red sunglasses. A used trolley pass. A parking ticket from the public lot on the south edge of town. A selfie with a police officer or firefighter—that one will be easy—one tourist map from the chamber of commerce office, two—"

Brady slammed on the brakes and Kate put a hand on the dashboard of the truck just as Brady reached over to keep her from jerking forward. His large hand rested on her shoulder, but her list of scavenger hunt items and her pen slid to the floor of the truck.

"Sorry," Brady said, pointing at the road in front of his truck. "Ducks. They're never in a hurry, waddling across the road."

A family of ducks slowly made their way across the street that lead through downtown Cape Pursuit. Traffic from the other direction had also stopped and she heard someone blow a horn. Kate glanced in the side mirror and recognized Holly's car behind them.

"We have tailgaters," she said. "Holly and Tom are right on our bumper. I wonder if they're going to follow us and piggyback on our success? I don't mind helping a friend, but she had her chance to have a great local partner like you and she blew it."

Kate wasn't at all sorry her roommate had decided to use the activity as a way to get Tom the Summer Heartbreaker's attention. If she had to run all over town with anyone, Kate was happy it was Brady. And, she had to admit, Brady was too nice of a guy to be stuck working with Holly, who was likely to lose interest or find something else to do before they were halfway through the list.

Brady grinned. "Do you want me to try to lose them?"

"No. We'll play nice at the mermaid statue while we pick up a brochure and take our picture, but we could employ some subterfuge and tell them we're going to go get coffee and take a break before we make any more stops on the scavenger hunt."

"Coffee sounds great," Brady said.

Kate swatted his shoulder playfully. "I was

kidding about that. We should knock out as many stops as we can early if we want a shot at winning this."

Brady ran a hand through his short hair and took his foot off the brake as the ducks finished crossing. He pulled into a parking spot in front of the coffee shop downtown, and Holly's car sped past them.

"What are you doing?" Kate asked.

"Giving them a head start. This way, we don't have to lie to them and we have the added bonus of doughnuts."

Kate almost protested at the way Brady had taken charge of their strategy, but she had to admit coffee and pastries sounded good. She nodded and took off her seat belt. "I see the wisdom of your plan. We fuel up, play it clean, and the victory will be even sweeter."

Brady smiled at her, their eyes lingering on each other, and Kate felt a wave of electricity run through her. If she were ever going to lose herself to a person or let herself fall into someone else's world, it would be with a man like Brady. *It would be Brady.* And that was exactly why he was so dangerous.

CHAPTER THIRTEEN

THE NEXT MORNING, Kate got up early even though she had been out late. It didn't have to be so late. She didn't have to take a walk on the beach and have a glass of wine with Brady at a beachfront bar after they had finished their scavenger hunt just before ten. She and Brady had checked off every item on the list, making sure to document their progress with numerous selfies on her phone. At the end of the summer, when she would leave for Florida, Kate would take with her at least twenty pictures of herself and Brady. They had used her phone each time with the intention of making it easy for one person to upload the results to the employee app. Kate was the more tech-savvy of the two, and she was happy to volunteer to be the keeper of the pictures.

Not that there was any other reason she wanted them. Her time with Brady was brief and sweet, like summer itself. She scrolled through the twenty pictures as she waited for her bagel to pop up. In one of them, she had her eyes closed. Brady had his eyes closed in another one. And a third picture had caught them both in an unprepared moment. She had a look of concentration on her face, but Brady was staring at her in the picture with an expression that was… She enlarged his face on her phone's screen. What was that look? Admiration? Friendship?

She didn't want to put a name on Brady's expression because it looked as if it went two steps beyond friendship and skipped right straight to something much deeper. He'd asked her to send him some of the pictures, and she would. But not that one.

A text pinged onto her phone.

Did we win?

Kate smiled.

I uploaded all our evidence, but no results yet. One hour to go.

See you there.

Although the pictures were turned in, participants in the scavenger hunt had to show up at eight and turn in the physical evidence of their success. Both parties had to be there, and Brady had traded part of a shift at the fire station to make sure he was available. Kate had felt bad asking him to do that, but he said he didn't mind owing someone a favor, especially if it meant a chance at a big win in the game. He'd also added he was happy to spend more time with her, but she hadn't responded to that. Would she sacrifice work time for him? She'd already refused to do that several times, and she needed to remember her priorities no matter how much fun it was to be with Brady.

Her future belonged to her.

Kate pulled into the office lot and parked next to Brady's truck. She hoped she'd see Holly's car. Her roommate hadn't come home the night before, and Kate wasn't sure what to conclude about it. Had she spent all night on the scavenger hunt with Tom? There had been no message from Holly and it wasn't the first time she hadn't come home for the night, but Kate had an uncomfortable feeling about her friend.

"Everything okay?" Brady asked as she got out of her car. He was waiting for her, both arms resting on the bedframe of his truck. "You look worried."

Kate shook her head. "I thought I'd see Holly's car here. She didn't come home last night."

Brady glanced at his watch. "She still has a few minutes. She seems like she might be a last-minute sort of person."

"That's a nice way of putting it," Kate said. "But Holly is a doesn't-always-come-through sort of person. One time last year, she was supposed to pick me up and she ended up going out with some guy."

"Just one time, though, right?" Brady said. *Does the guy want to think the best of everyone?*

"It was pouring down rain that night," Kate said. "And it happened twice after that until I finally learned my lesson."

"Sounds like Holly is good at training her friends," Brady said. "That's a useful skill, I guess."

Kate laughed. "I just wish she was good at choosing the right friends. Or even just learning to trust and like herself. She'd be happier."

Being around Holly every day reminded Kate that personal relationships could be like bumpy pothole-filled streets and that taking to the smooth lonely sidewalk had a greater chance of leading to happiness. Kate chose her own way because she knew she was the one person who would never let her down and she was the one thing in life over which she had total control.

Brady smiled at her in the morning sunshine and Kate's heart flashed into traitor territory for a moment. She took a deep breath and got out her phone so she could focus on something practical. "I'll send you some of those pictures while we're waiting for the office to open and George to crown a winner."

Kate and Brady walked over to the area outside the office door where the teams had gathered the previous morning. There were only about three-quarters of the people that had been there the day before.

"Did we have some dropouts and nonfinishers?" Brady asked. "It was tough, but not that tough."

Kate have him a little shrug as she scrolled through pictures. Brady leaned in and looked at her phone.

"Of course, I was blessed with the best partner, so who am I to judge other teams for giving up in miserable defeat or sitting down and having ice cream on the beach instead of continuing the hunt?" he said. "Wait," he added, pointing to a picture on her screen. "Will you make sure to send me that one? I look like a goofball, but I love the way you're smiling at me, anyway."

Kate had been so busy looking at Brady in all the pictures that she hadn't noticed herself. *Oh, goodness.* The picture he was pointing at was of the two of them sitting on the sand. In the photo, Kate held out her hand, palm up, showing the beach glass they had found, but she was looking at Brady. And the look on her face showed every symptom of the attraction he tempted her with.

"It's supposed to be about the beach glass," she said, trying to keep her voice as level and practical as possible.

"It wasn't about—" Brady began, but Holly trooped up alongside Kate and hip-checked her.

"Made it," she said. "Bet you were doubting."

Holly's hair was ruffled and a flake of old mascara was stuck to her cheek, but she looked happy. Kate hoped she'd been beachcombing or sea turtle hunting all night, or had even been engaged in a long board game or Uno battle. Kate knew Holly had a lot of friends aside from herself, so she had probably been just fine wherever she spent the night.

"Did you and Tom get everything on the list?" Kate asked.

Holly leaned in and whispered, "Officially, yes, but we may have fudged a few things."

Kate swallowed, not wanting to say anything negative. It was only a game and not worth arguing over. Not worth cheating over, either, but she decided to keep her opinion to herself. Kate glanced at Brady to gauge his reaction, but he had his hands in his pockets and his eyes on the ground, revealing nothing. Kate didn't know everything about his character, but she would have bet her car that he was a man who hated cheating, even if he forgave the cheaters.

"Great news," George said, greeting the crowd outside his office. "We had fourteen teams compete in the first ever company scavenger hunt, and everyone earned points. The top prize of five hundred bonus points is going to be tougher to award than I thought.

Believe it or not, there were five teams that completed all the items on the list and are eligible for the grand prize. So, you're going to have a tough choice to make."

George named off the five teams, which included Kate and Brady and Holly and Tom. All the teams stepped forward and waited. Kate felt a flutter of nervousness. Were they going to have to compete with each other? Couldn't George just award five prizes?

"I could divide the points evenly among you," George continued, "one hundred each. Or we could draw names out of a hat and choose one winner. I don't want to hand five hundred points to each team because it will inflate the values so much that other teams might be inclined to give up. I'll give you a minute to discuss it."

Brady turned to Kate. "I'd be happy with the one hundred each. Hate to turn down a sure thing and gamble away points."

Kate had been thinking exactly the opposite. Her first instinct was to play for the big prize and take her chances. She shouldn't be at all surprised that Brady wanted to play it safe. He was a play-it-safe kind of guy—as if she needed one more reminder. Before Kate

replied to Brady with her opinion, she over-
heard the other teams discussing it with almost all the opinions going for a nice safe
split. Holly was the only dissenter.

"You're with me, right, Kate? Go big or go
home?" Holly said. Kate cared for her friend,
and she had to admit her first instinct was exactly Holly's, but she had to choose sides and
Holly's competitive ethics weren't looking
very good in the morning light. Would Kate
rather please Holly or Brady? Which choice
would please herself—a measure she had always relied on since she became an adult and
made her own decisions.

Kate flicked a glance at Brady with his patient smile, and she slowly shook her head at
Holly. "I'm content to take my share of the
points and go start my shift driving the trolley. Some points are better than no points."

The eight-hour trolley shift was going to
be a welcome diversion because she needed
time at the wheel to sort out her complicated
feelings. Torn between choosing Holly's good
opinion or Brady's, she'd chosen him and settled for the sure thing. Was that what people
did in relationships? Settle for safety?

Brady was smiling at her as if she had just

handed him a whole sky full of stars, and Kate didn't know what to say to him. She wasn't perfect and she certainly wasn't perfect for him. When he looked at her with his warm chocolate eyes and contented smile, it reminded her how much she was going to disappoint him at the end of the summer when she did exactly what she'd been telling him she was going to do. Did he believe she would really leave? Sometimes he didn't act like it.

"It's five after eight," Kate told Brady, pointing at the time on her cell phone. "So I'm five minutes late getting the trolley on its circuit. Go ahead and enter my vote for splitting the prize, and I'll talk with you later."

"I'll call you," he said, his hand rubbing her upper arm and leaving a trail of warmth. "But I'm doing a twelve-hour shift starting this evening."

She nodded and smiled. "Be careful," she said, and then she went into the office to clock in for a shift, taking people wherever they wanted to go while she thought about all the places she hoped to go.

BRADY GOT OFF work at seven the next morning, went home and logged into his email on his computer. His brother told him he should set up his phone to receive emails and he would never have to worry about getting messages hours later, but Brady didn't usually see the big deal.

Unless he was waiting for important news like his preapproval from the bank. It had been a week since he applied, and the bank had promised an email by today. But it was early in the morning, before the bank opened. Nothing interesting awaited him in the in-box—just the usual offers of discount travel, unsolicited requests for insurance or prescription medications and advertisements from the places where he'd purchased black shoes for work and new floor mats for his truck.

One email from the bank could change his life. He could drive by that perfect blue house with the tree in the front yard and feel that—perhaps—his dream was close enough to touch. He'd already waited a long time, and it looked as if he was going to have to wait until at least later in the afternoon when he got home from his second, but necessary, job.

He tried to shake off his disappointment as he put on his Cape Pursuit Trolley shirt and shorts. He padded into his kitchen barefoot and made a quick peanut butter sandwich and tossed it in a bag with a bottle of water and a bag of chips. The eight-to-four shift driving the trolley was his favorite, but he already knew he wouldn't be working with his favorite coworker. Kate was in the office during the day and then scheduled to drive from four to midnight—a shift that got pretty lonely after the sun went down, but Kate didn't seem to mind.

As he drove throughout the day, he thought about his brother's advice and wished he had taken it. He could have pulled out his phone at a trolley stop or during his quick lunch. Every time they passed a house along the route or he caught sight of a for-sale sign down one of the side streets, the flicker of excitement about his loan application took his thoughts straight to the blue house. No matter how many friendly tourists and cute kids got on the trolley, his heart was elsewhere on the long torturous day of waiting. When he finally parked the trolley a few minutes before four and saw Kate coming across the parking lot, his joy at seeing his replacement driver was even stronger than usual. There had to be an email waiting for him at home. He could know within fifteen minutes.

He bounded out of the seat, ready to greet Kate with a kiss in the empty trolley, but Kate's expression as she came up the steps was a wet blanket on a campfire.

"Is everything okay?" he asked, immediately forgetting his email and taking Kate's hand. "You look upset."

Kate glanced around the trolley, clearly checking to make sure they were alone. "It's Holly."

"Is she all right?" Brady asked. He'd been on duty at the station all day and there hadn't been any accidents involving a young woman.

Kate swallowed and laced her fingers together. "Basically, yes, but she's in a bit of trouble. She met a guy." Kate sighed. "At the bar last night, and she left town with him this morning for some stupid reason I don't know, and—long story short—he dumped her about two hours away from here."

A hundred worried thoughts raced through Brady's mind. "But you said she's okay."

Kate nodded. "I think so. But someone needs to go get her."

"I'll go with you."

Kate looped an arm around him and laid her head on his chest. Brady cautiously put his arms around her and held her in a close hug. This was a new side of Kate he'd never seen, the Kate who reached out and needed someone, even though she was asking for a friend and not herself.

"Someone has to drive this trolley tonight. I'm scheduled, but—"

"Tell me what you need me to do. I can take your shift here, or I can go pick up Holly. Your choice."

He was sure he was looking at eight more hours of driving and eight more hours of wondering about his email in-box, but he would do it without a second of complaint.

Kate backed away and looked up at Brady. "I saw the guy she was with. I…didn't like the look of him."

"I'll go."

"I…wish you would, even though I hate asking. If things go well, you'll be there and back in just four hours and you'll get to bed at a decent time," Kate said. "I know you must be tired after working last night at the station and all day here." Her eyebrows came together and formed a line. "I don't know who else to ask."

Brady ran a hand over her hair. "I'm always here for you."

Kate pressed a set of car keys into his hand. "Take my car. I just filled it up this morning, even though I had no idea I'd need to take a road trip today."

"I'll drive my truck. Just text me the address."

"I don't want you to have to do that—"

Brady smiled. "Do you think my truck smells too funny inside for your friend?"

Kate almost laughed, and the line between her eyebrows smoothed out. Brady hated seeing her upset and he wished he could clear the way for her wherever she went even though she would hate that.

"I'm sorry about this," she said.

Brady kissed her on the lips and lingered there just long enough to wish he didn't have to go. "Don't be. I'll let you know when I've found her, and I may even let her buy me dinner at a drive-through on the way back."

Kate fumbled in her purse. "She won't have any money, I'm sure. She—"

Brady caught her hands. "I'm kidding. I'll call you."

He gave her back her car keys, clocked out in the office and headed for his truck. His email could wait. Before he started his truck, his phone pinged with a message from Kate with the address of a roadside restaurant a good two hours west of Cape Pursuit. It would be a long evening, and he had no idea what he and Holly were going to talk about on the two-hour ride home, but he knew one thing for certain.

Kate had needed help, and she had come to him. That would give him plenty to think about on the road. Brady headed west, and he did think about Kate along the way, but he also thought about Holly and what motivated her to choose the wrong kind of guys and trust them. He knew her type, sadly. Had grown up with a mother who wasn't a bad person, just as Holly wasn't, but who made profoundly bad choices. At least Holly didn't have any kids depending on her, and she had something his mother didn't. She had a good friend who tried to keep her out of trouble and was quick to help her when she needed it. What would happen to Holly when she and Kate parted ways at the end of the summer?

What would happen to him?

After Brady pulled into the roadside restaurant and went inside, he found Holly at a booth by the window, scrolling through screens on her phone.

"Where's Kate?" she asked as soon as Brady slid into the booth across from her.

"Working. I had the evening off and I volunteered to come pick you up and give you a lift home," he said, being careful not to let any judgment creep into his voice. Growing up as he did, he knew darn well that he and his brother, Noah, could easily have fallen into a messy lifestyle filled with destructive decisions. Noah had been saved by Corrinne's love and now his responsibility as a father to Bella, and Brady had been saved by that protective voice inside him that drove him to help others instead of becoming a burden himself.

Holly swallowed. "Sorry," she said. Her eyes became watery and Brady pulled a napkin from the holder on the empty table.

"It's okay. Listen, I'm starving, so why don't I get us both some dinner and then we'll get home in time for the sunset in Cape Pursuit."

Holly nodded. Brady ordered them both a sandwich platter and glasses of soda, and they ate in silence and then got in the truck.

After a half hour of near silence, Holly asked, "You're not going to say anything about how stupid I am?"

Brady shook his head. "You're not any stupider than the rest of us. You trusted your heart a little sooner than you should have, but there's no harm done. Is there?" he said, looking at her with concern.

"No harm," she said. "I've been thinking… well, I think maybe it's time I go home. My sister works at a nice salon in Tulsa, does hair and nails. She took a beauty course at the community college, and my parents want me to come back and maybe go into business with Annie."

"That sounds like a good plan," Brady offered.

He heard her let out a long shuddering breath. "I wasn't good enough for any of the boys I went to high school with," she said. "I thought I'd get away and meet new people, meet a decent guy."

Brady let silence fill the cab of his truck for another mile. "I grew up with a single mom who went from one abusive relationship to the next and she dragged my brother and me right along with her," Brady said. "She never thought she was good enough for any of those guys, and she let them walk all over her."

"That must have been awful."

"I learned a lot from the experience," he said. "And it wasn't all bad."

He wanted to tell her he hoped she learned to value herself so she'd stop the pattern she'd begun to establish, but she didn't need his lectures. She needed a safe ride home.

"Hope Kate's not too mad at me," Holly said. "She always seems to know what she wants. Like pilot school."

Brady suppressed a smile. "I think she wants to be a flight attendant, not a pilot, even though I'm sure she would be a good one."

"Oh, I guess I wasn't listening when she told me about that school she's going to." Holly blew out a sigh. "She's a much better friend than I am."

"She is a good friend," he said slowly. Despite the unbalanced relationship with Holly.

And where was the balance in his relationship with Kate? He knew he wanted more than she was willing to give, and at the end of the summer, he would be the one who was much more disappointed and sorry to see the season fade away. Kate didn't ask much of him, no matter how badly he wanted to give her his time and his heart.

Were all relationships fated to be uneven? He set the cruise control on his truck so he would have one less thing to think about as he drove toward Cape Pursuit. Holly leaned her head against the passenger window and fell asleep, and he had only his thoughts to keep him company. He'd watched his mother try to be good enough for various men for years, and he'd fallen into the same trap himself for a long time—always trying to be the perfect son and fill up some gap he couldn't measure.

Firefighting had given him confidence and purpose and shown him that he didn't have to be in a race to prove himself. He had Noah and Bella, and that would be enough. They would be there when Kate left to chase her dreams at summer's end. All he had to do was make sure he protected his heart from any lasting damage.

CHAPTER FOURTEEN

THE OCEANSIDE RESTAURANT was definitely a dinner-date venue. All around Kate and Brady, couples were talking or holding hands over glasses of wine or craft beer. Because it was a beautiful warm evening with just the right amount of ocean breeze, Kate and Brady sat on the patio where they could sometimes distinguish the sounds of the ocean and the cry of seagulls over the sounds of their fellow diners.

"I'm buying dinner tonight," Kate said. "To thank you for picking up Holly on your evening off yesterday. I'm sure you had something better in mind for your night."

Brady reached across the table and rubbed the back of Kate's hand lightly with two fingers. "I didn't mind, but I'm much happier with this evening and being here with you."

Kate smiled and nodded. She didn't know what to say. Of course she had agreed to dinner with Brady, had even been relieved that she could thank him in a tangible way for helping out her friend. And they were—sort of—dating. Even a no-strings summer romance included sunset dinners, walks on the beach, kisses that lingered with the pink and gold streaks in the sky.

She extracted her hand from Brady's touch by picking up her menu with both hands. All the food looked tempting and wonderful and she doubted it was possible to make a bad choice. She swallowed and tried to focus on the list of entrees and details about sides so she wouldn't have to face the temptation across the table. Not that Brady was a bad choice. If she was going to join her heart and her emotions to another human, there weren't many men as strong, capable, appealing... lovable...as Brady. And that was exactly why she needed to remember her goals. *Her* goals.

"Confession," Brady said. "I live in an oceanfront town, but I don't like seafood."

"No seafood at all?"

He shrugged and gave a half smile. "I'm probably not supposed to admit to liking those breaded fish sticks that come in a cardboard box in the freezer section."

"No one admits that, but I think it's a more common guilty pleasure than you might think. You're allowed."

Brady blew out a sigh that sounded like relief. "Combined with mac and cheese, also from a cardboard box, that was one of my mother's specialties. Not that I blame her, because I think she was doing the best she could. I didn't learn to cook from her, but I'm an adult now, so there's nothing stopping me from being a decent cook except time and bravery."

Kate laughed. "I can see where you don't have time, but I doubt you lack bravery."

"Are you kidding? Kitchen fires are a menace. I'm not sure it's worth the risk. Not when there are nice places like this," he said, opening his hand in a small wave that encompassed the restaurant's patio. "And they don't just serve seafood."

"I'm going to have the pasta," Kate said. "I'm fueling up for a late night of Uber driving, which is why I'm insanely jealous of that beer you're having."

"You could take a night off. We could have too many drinks and call an Uber to take us home in the ultimate display of irony."

Kate smiled. "When was the last time you had too much to drink or did anything reckless at all?"

"I go into burning buildings on a fairly regular basis."

"That's not reckless. My guess is that you're perfectly in control," Kate said.

"No one is perfectly in control, especially when you're battling a force of nature, but I do wear my flame retardant underwear, just in case." Brady grinned at her and the rays of the sunset lit one side of his face and left the other in shadow. Brady didn't have a dark side—at least, none that Kate could see—but she knew his childhood hadn't been all sunshine. His thirst for a solid home was part of that, but in other ways he seemed to have completely transcended what was behind him.

They ordered their dinners and Brady sat back and sipped his beer. "I'm celebrating a small victory tonight."

"The scavenger hunt? That victory ended up being a lot smaller than I thought it would be."

He shook his head. "Something bigger. My Realtor, Charlie, who is also a firefighter, talked me into going to the bank and doing the paperwork to get preapproved for a home loan. I thought it was wild advice because I didn't believe I had close to enough money or that I was worth much at all."

Kate scoffed. "You're worth a lot."

He smiled broadly. "I know that now. And I have proof. The bank says I'm worth taking a chance on."

Brady was a truthful and even humble person, quick to help others, thoughtful...but definitely too risky for her to take a chance on. He was the kind of person who would be hard to forget no matter how many miles she traveled.

"I'm talking about a mortgage," Brady said, dipping his chin and giving her a sideways smile. "You looked pretty worried there for a minute, like you thought I was going to raffle myself off to the highest bidder on the beach."

Kate laughed. "Congratulations on your preapproval."

"Thanks. It makes me less worried, but now I also feel more pressure. It's strange, when something you thought was out of reach for so long seems to be suddenly within reach. It's scary because you don't want to screw it up."

"You won't."

He raised his eyebrows and cocked his head. "How do you know? I have no experience as a homeowner. Maybe I'll be lousy at it. What if I'm the guy who accidentally destroys his lawn by using too much fertilizer or mowing it way too short and the entire neighborhood goes down the drain? I could be that guy who doesn't know which day is garbage collection day and leaves his cans on the curb all week."

Kate shook her head. "You paint a grim picture of failure, but I think you're worrying over nothing. Do you manage to take care of your lawn and successfully handle garbage day now?"

"Yes. But the stakes will be higher with my own place."

"You'll survive," Kate said. "Maybe your brother will help you."

"Maybe. I wish I knew his long-range plan. There's nothing I'd like more than having him and Bella under my roof."

Kate imagined herself under his roof for just the briefest moment. Standing next to him in the kitchen waiting for the toast to pop up, leaving her shoes by the front door, her towel on the rack in the bathroom. She took a big gulp of her raspberry iced tea to wash away the thought.

"So, when do you buy this dream house?" she asked.

"I've picked out a few that I want to go back and look at now that I know I just might be able to get one of them. I'll have to sign a million forms that will probably scare me to death, but I hope to move on this soon so I might be in my own place by Christmas."

Kate remembered Christmas growing up. It had been almost smothering in its perfection. Carefully decorated cookies. Just the right tree that filled the space in the front window. Stacked gifts under the tree in three different coordinated wrapping papers. Candles. Turkey. Grandparents. Perfect. But it had also been exactly the same every year, choreographed right down to the last minute. The tiny skaters in their musical snow globe always got the same spot on the shelf over the fireplace and three embroidered stockings hung in their assigned places year after year. They'd had to *wait for her father to get home* every year so he could put the star on top of the tree.

It was—sort of—a nice memory now that she thought of it, and it was nice that her father was tall enough to put the star on top and he was always there right when they needed him. Kate took a deep breath of ocean air. If she went back home to her parents, or if she tied her life to a homebody like Brady, it would mean ties where she wanted freedom. She didn't want to see the same paint colors in every room year after year or put the dishes back in their exact place in the kitchen cabinet. She wanted change and the freedom that came with it.

"Christmas," she said lightly. "I could be anywhere by then."

Brady's expression flickered from happiness to sadness for a moment and then his bright smile returned. "You could celebrate aboard a flight to some amazing European city where they invented Christmas trees or someplace tropical with steel drums instead of jingle bells."

"Or someplace way up north where snow comes from," she said playfully. "Well, maybe not. I don't want to freeze while I'm on a sleigh ride."

"That's the beauty of Cape Pursuit. I can put up Christmas lights without ever having to battle snow and ice."

Their dinners arrived and smelled delicious. Somehow, thinking about Christmas had made her feel an unwelcome nostalgia. She was a person who always looked forward…but, strangely, so was Brady. His looking-forward plans were a whole lot different from hers—him taking solace from a roof and four walls, her finding herself in open skies.

"It sounds like you've got it all planned out," Kate commented.

"As much as anyone does."

"Speaking of people who plan and people who don't," Kate said. "Holly and I talked for a long time last night when I got home from work."

Brady chewed a piece of steak, his eyes on her, waiting for her to go on.

"She said you two had talked in the truck and you mentioned that your mom didn't… always…have her plan together."

Brady swallowed and took a sip of beer. "I

don't think she ever had her plan together. We loved her, anyway, just like you care about Holly no matter how much she tests your friendship."

"She's flying home tomorrow," Kate said. "Back to Tulsa. Can you believe I didn't even know that was where she was from? I guess we didn't talk about our past much."

"You don't," Brady commented.

Kate didn't take the bait. She and Brady had a here-and-now relationship, and there was no way he would understand that a suffocating and perfect childhood motivated her in a similar and ironic way to how a nomadic one seemed to mark him.

"I know what I'm doing tomorrow," she said. "I'm taking her to the airport, even though I had to give up an overtime shift I was planning to work."

"Nice of you."

"I should have gone yesterday instead of sending you. I want to do this for her since who knows when I'll ever see her again?"

Kate was surprised at the emotion that crept into her voice and the faint stinging in her eyes. She was not a sentimental person who clung to people or places. She didn't want to be that person whose life was a bomb shelter filled with safe choices.

"Off to the airport," Brady said cheerfully. "A glimpse into your future. And you never did tell me all about your visit to the flight attendant school. I know what the fire academy was like, but I don't know about the training you'll have to go through. Do you get to use the emergency slide?"

Happy to have a change of subject, Kate worked her way through a plate of pasta while telling Brady all about the courses she would take: the rules of airline travel and the finer points of luggage restrictions and running the ticket counter.

"What about fire safety? What kind of fire suppression systems do the different aircraft have?" he asked.

Kate lifted one shoulder in a small shrug. "I don't know yet. That's one of the things I'll have to learn."

Even though she'd be miles away without any intention of coming back to Cape Pursuit, she knew she would think of Brady every time fire safety came up in her classes. It was a good thing she was walking away from him in a few months before he got any deeper under her skin.

BRADY PULLED THE main pumper out of the station and parked it on the wide front apron. He got out and put the wheel chocks in place, kicking them for good measure to make sure they were tight and the truck wouldn't roll. A kid went by on her bicycle and Brady waved to her, wondering if she'd grow up to be a firefighter. He headed back into the station to pull out another truck so they could hose down the interior floor, but movement on the sidewalk caught his eye.

Kate.

He strode across the concrete to meet her. "Nice surprise," he said, wondering if it would be appropriate to kiss her while at work in plain view. The other firefighters were in the station, some of them moving trucks and some doing a preliminary sweep of the floor for its weekly scrub down.

"I'm afraid I'm starting to be a pest," she said. "I should have called first."

He caught her hand. "What do you need?"

"To borrow your truck."

"Okay."

Kate laughed. "Aren't you even going to ask why?"

"I already know why. You said you needed it, and that's good enough for me."

He just wished he was good enough that Kate would see he was worth a long-term relationship and not the half-measure bound-for-disappointment summer romance they were currently having.

"My car is sort of out of commission this morning."

"Won't start?"

She shook her head. He tightened his grip on her hand with a sudden streak of worry. "You didn't have an accident last night while you were driving people around, did you?"

He would have heard about it for certain if anything had happened to her within the Cape Pursuit Fire Department's jurisdiction.

"No. At least, not the kind you're thinking of. I took some passengers home way after midnight from the bar and one of them puked in the back of my car. I thought I had it cleaned out last night, but after sitting overnight with the windows up, the smell almost knocked me back ten feet when I opened the door this morning."

Brady smiled. "Want to borrow my air freshener?"

"I think only time and fresh air is going to help that problem."

Brady reached into his pocket and pulled out his truck keys. "It's all yours. I'll be here until at least seven tonight, so I won't miss it."

"It's only two hours to Richmond, but Holly'll probably want me to hang out with her until she has to go through security and out to her gate. She's nervous about flying."

"Take your time."

He trusted Kate completely with his vehicle. She was an excellent driver—something he knew from experience working with her—and she was truthful with him and her other friends. He didn't worry about the truck, but he did worry that seeing her friend off at the airport might inspire Kate to move up her own departure plans. She loved being on the road. Would going to an airport and watching someone else take off make her want to do the same?

Kate took the keys from his outstretched palm and let her fingers graze his wrist. If only he could pull her close and hold on until she changed her mind about always wanting to run away.

He swallowed and fought the emotion that

came from the simple act of handing her a set of keys as if he was handing her freedom. "Wish Holly the best for me," he said.

She nodded, a serious expression on her lovely face. "I wish I knew how it was going to work out for her. Going home." She shook her head. "I hope it's what she really wants."

"Be careful," Brady said.

"I'll bring your truck back without a scratch."

"I don't give a damn about the truck. But I'll be looking forward to seeing you."

Kate looked into his eyes for a long time without moving and Brady almost lost the battle about kissing her when she suddenly touched her fingers to her own lips and then to his before turning and walking toward the parking lot.

As if the gods of public safety wanted to torture him, it was one of the slowest days in the history of the department. There were no false alarms. No fires. Only one tiny fender bender for which they were canceled before they even rolled out of the station. *She should be getting back. It had been about five hours.* Brady took all the furniture out of the break room. Every folding table, every chair. He stacked them neatly and scrubbed the walls and floor.

When he finished inside, he attacked the gutters. How had a department with easy access to ladders allowed so many leaves to settle into their rain gutters? He climbed onto the department's roof with an empty five-gallon bucket and scooped leaves out of the gutters. *It had been almost seven hours now. Was Kate okay? Had she gotten on a plane, too?* He had to climb down from the roof several times and empty his bucket, each time enjoying the satisfaction of doing something beneficial. And keeping his thoughts from driving him crazy.

"What kind of trouble is chasing you today?"

Brady glanced down at the ground as he stepped onto the top of the ladder with his last bucket of leaves. He'd scooped the gutters on all sides of the building completely clean. Tony was below, shading his eyes as he looked up.

"Just staying busy, Chief," Brady said. "Nobody seems to need us today."

"That's a good thing."

Brady backed down the ladder and put his bucket of leaves on the ground.

"Something under your skin?" Tony asked.

Brady shrugged. It was nothing he could put into words even though he considered Tony a friend. He knew Tony had struggled with his relationship with Laura. He would probably understand what it was like to want someone you couldn't have, but what was the use of bellyaching about something he'd brought on himself? He *could* have kept his distance from Kate from the start instead of letting himself fall into the habit of hoping for something that would never happen. That's what he *should* have done, but then he would have missed out on precious time with her that would never come around again.

"I came out to tell you your friend Kate is back with your truck. She just pulled into the lot."

"Thanks," Brady said.

Tony took the bucket. "I've got this. And I'll put the ladder away, too. You've done more than your share today and you can go ahead and leave. It's almost time, and there's nothing going on here."

"Thanks," Brady repeated, hoping he could spend the evening with Kate.

Brady walked through the station and found Kate standing out front. She held out his keys and he took them wordlessly, a thousand questions reeling through his head.

"I'm sorry I was gone for so long. Her flight was delayed and she wanted me to stay. She's on her way to Tulsa with one stopover in Chicago," Kate said.

"Have you been to both those places?" Brady was sure Kate had been nearly everywhere. It was, honestly, a miracle that she'd come back to Cape Pursuit for the summer. Couldn't she have made her tuition money at any number of slightly-over-minimum-wage jobs? Was there something else that had brought her back? He knew she would never admit it if there were, and it didn't matter, anyway, because nothing in Cape Pursuit was going to hold her there.

"More than once," Kate said. "But I wasn't sightseeing. I was driving the truck, moving on to my next destination."

"I'm glad you're back," he said, knowing he meant back in Cape Pursuit for the summer and also back from her trip to the Richmond airport. She'd only been gone about seven hours, but it had seemed like two days. How was he going to cope when she left for good in September? If luck was on his side, he could put his energy into a new house.

"Me, too. I forgot my sunglasses and I'm ready to give my eyes a rest."

Brady felt a wave of the frustration that had been simmering under his skin all day. "I know that you…that we…" He rocked back on his heels and looked up at the early-evening sky. The sun was still bright, and he was sure Kate was being truthful about her tired eyes. But couldn't he be forgiven for wanting something more?

"I'm not just glad to be back because I'm tired of driving," Kate said. She stepped closer and, even though they weren't physically touching, Brady felt connected to her in a way that was sure to hurt when the connection inevitably broke. "I'm glad to see you."

He smiled, the tension leaving his body with just a few little words from her. "I was serious when I said I didn't care about that truck. But I was afraid you'd keep driving once you got on the road," he admitted. "I know you love your independence, and this is just a temporary stop—"

Kate put her hand on his upper arm. "I have no plans to leave before I said I would at the end of the summer."

Relief washed through him like a cool drink on a hot day.

"In fact, I was thinking about you most of the way home."

"You were?"

"I think if we team up, we both have a better chance of winning the grand prize in the employee challenge. We could even make a deal. If either one of us wins it, we agree to split it with the other one."

Brady swallowed. She was sticking around for the rest of the summer because of a silly game and a shot at winning it. Was that all he meant to her? Not that she'd promised him anything else.

"That sounds like a win-win," he said. "Can't lose." He smiled, but he didn't feel like smiling inside. He'd chuck the whole stupid game just for a chance at something lasting with Kate.

"Are you busy tonight?" she asked.

He shook his head. "Just leaving, but

I wouldn't mind a shower and change of clothes. Did you have something in mind?" Even if she broke his heart by saying she wanted to compare notes and progress in the online game, he knew he'd be too weak to say no. He'd take whatever scraps she offered and store them up against a fall and winter of loneliness.

"Nothing special. I thought maybe we could go somewhere where the lights aren't too bright," she said, shading her eyes from the sun. "You could tell me about your day and I could buy you dinner as a thank-you for lending me your excellent-smelling truck."

"Is fire station smell growing on you?"

"More than I should admit," she said.

Brady's heart took a risky leap at her words, but he reminded himself to keep the evening in perspective. His relationship with Kate had an expiration date that wasn't going to change.

CHAPTER FIFTEEN

KATE PUT ON her Cape Pursuit Trolley hat and reflected on the fact that Brady Adams always seemed to be close by. When she agreed to drive the trolley in the annual Cape Pursuit Fourth of July Parade, she didn't know a massive fire truck would be right behind her in the lineup. And she certainly couldn't have predicted Brady would be the driver of that truck. Had he traded someone else just to be right behind her?

"Try not to scare me," Kate told Brady as they waited in a large parking lot that was the staging area for the parade.

"I doubt I could even if I wanted to," Brady said.

Kate laughed. "Okay, I mean try not to startle me. I have the lives of a dozen summer workers in my hands."

"I'll only blow the air horn when it's absolutely necessary," Brad said.

"What would necessitate that?"

Brady blew out a breath and crossed his arms over his broad chest. "Well, I'd have to blow the horn if I saw someone I knew along the route."

"Which is everybody."

"Not everybody, but more than ten. And I'd pull the air horn if a little kid ran into the road for candy and I needed to warn him or her."

"Acceptable," Kate agreed.

"And, of course, anyone with an air horn is obligated to make some noise if someone makes the universal air horn gesture." Brady demonstrated the bent-elbow pull-down that meant the same thing all across the country. Kate had encountered it plenty during her time as a truck driver. She had seldom accommodated any requests because she generally tried to avoid bringing attention to herself. Flying under and outside the radar worked for her as a single woman in a solitary job, and pretty soon she'd be doing a whole different kind of flying.

The thought took her away from Cape Pursuit for a moment as she imagined spending her time in the skies instead of on the confining highways.

"Just stick with the program and snake along with the other poor suckers driving in this," Brady said. "I did it last year and I only survived it because I kept swiping candy out of the bucket."

Kate laughed. "I'll make all my riders share." She knew there would be astounding quantities of candy onboard the trolley for the summer workers to toss out the windows. Kate had ordered the candy herself based on the notes left from the previous secretary. All the volunteers on the trolley would earn bonus points in the employee game, and Kate was glad she was getting points, too. She had missed the parade the previous summer because she'd taken a shift working George's ice cream stand near the beach. This year, she would ring the trolley bell all along the parade route.

She was glad her boss had given her the job of driving the trolley. Creeping along the streets of Cape Pursuit at parade speed would be agonizing with someone else at the wheel. All she had to do was keep an adequate distance between the trolley and the vehicle ahead of her. The car ahead of the trolley was a restored 1930s-era Auburn with big, sweeping fenders and an air of drama. It had flag buntings on the side and carried the parade's royalty. Kate was already dreading watching the parade queen wave mechanically all along the parade route. What fun could that possibly be for the girl? Sure, she wore a sparkling red dress and had perfect pageant hair, but Kate would rather be driving the trolley or anything else instead of being put on display.

"I'll see you at the end," Brady said. "We'll both have to get our vehicles off the streets, but then I hope you're still planning to come to the family picnic."

A family picnic. Brady and his brother were taking Bella to the park for an early-afternoon picnic after the parade, and Kate had said yes even though she felt she might be intruding. Her family had never picnicked. Eating on the veranda outside their dining room two or three times a summer had been as close to a dining adventure as her mother was willing to tolerate. They had their assigned places at the dining room table, and her mother hadn't seen any reason to alter those places.

"Sure," Kate said, trying to muster enthusiasm. "I mean, there's always a chance George will need me for something with this being such a busy day, but I'm officially off between the parade and my driving shift starting at four."

"Good." Brady smiled. "Bella was excited when I told her the trolley lady would be at our picnic, and Noah would like a chance to get to know you."

"Why?" The word was out of her mouth before she considered it.

"Because you're a friend of mine," Brady said. His eyebrows drew together as if he was looking at a puzzle, but then his face relaxed and his smile returned. "It's just a picnic, Kate. Not a marriage proposal."

Words stuck in her throat at the obvious but still jarring joke, and Kate was thrilled to hear a police siren signaling the start of the parade. Without another word, she left Brady standing next to a massive and shiny fire truck and she dove onto the trolley to take refuge behind the driver's seat. *Marriage proposal.* What on earth had even made him say such a ridiculous thing?

Behind her, twelve summer workers lined up, six per side at open windows with buckets of candy. Kate rang the bell and prepared to crawl along despite how much she wanted to put her foot through the floorboard and speed away.

A siren blared behind her and she heard three sharp blasts of an air horn. In front of her, the parade queen began an agonizingly slow royal wave. Kate couldn't see her face, but she knew that poor girl had a plastered-on smile no matter how hot she felt in her sparkling dress. By the end of the long parade route, the queen would probably want to jump on Kate's trolley and escape, too.

Kate started driving, keeping her prescribed distance from the car ahead, and didn't look at the crowd.

"Chocolate?" Josh asked as he held out his bucket. "Whoever picked this out got the good stuff, but it will melt fast on a hot day like today."

Kate flashed a quick smile at her coworker and returned her eyes to the pageant queen ahead. "Just one piece," she said as she dipped into the bucket without looking. She carefully unwrapped the candy while keeping most of her fingers on the wheel and took a bite. While on the road as a cross-country truck driver, she'd kept to a strict no-eating-behind-the-wheel rule. She was afraid that once she started snacking on those long lonely miles, she might never stop. This was different. Everything was different. Temptation in Cape Pursuit came in another form.

The fire siren blared an up-down wail just as she thought of Brady. Little kids clapped their hands over their ears but stood up and looked at the truck behind Kate as if it was a magical dragon.

"I think we're getting passed by ants," Josh said as he stood in the open doorway and tossed candy to kids. "This is going to be a melty mess if you don't step on it."

Kate laughed, but there wasn't a thing she could do except pity the parade queen ahead of her who was baking in the open car.

After the parade, Kate dropped off her passengers and the trolley. The auto detailer had gotten the funk out of her car, but she left it under a shade tree in the lot at the office and decided to walk to the park instead. The streets were clogged with people leaving the parade route, and she was tired of being confined. She thought she'd beaten Brady to the park, but she saw him hop out of the fire truck and then someone else drove it away.

Of course, he had a plan. And there was no avoiding him because he saw Kate as soon as his feet hit the sidewalk.

"We're meeting by the fountain," he said as he approached. "My brother has our blanket and food, but don't get your hopes up on the food. I wasn't very creative with the sandwiches and chips."

"I'm sure it'll be great," Kate said.

Brady put an arm around her shoulders and turned her toward the fountain where they'd meet his family—more spokes in the wheel of relationships she was trying to avoid.

BRADY OFFERED THE last prepackaged cupcake to Kate, Bella and then his brother, but they all turned it down. Even after a sandwich and a small bag of chips, he was still hungry, so Brady was happy to have the last dessert. It could be a long night at the station and who knew when his next meal would be? "You're all missing out on the best desserts the convenience store near my house had, but I'll finish off the box if you want." It would have been nice to actually bake something and maybe even have Bella help. He wished he could remember helping his mom in the kitchen, licking the icing off a spoon, smelling birthday cakes rising in the oven.

No matter how many hours he spent at work, he would help Noah make a birthday cake for Bella and let her help ice it. The future was going to be different.

"You can have it," Noah said. "Bella and I already had a bunch of parade candy, so our teeth are in the danger zone." He sucked in his lips and made a funny face that made him look as if he had no teeth and his daughter laughed. Brady laughed, too, and he was pleased to see Kate smile and chuckle. Was she having a good time? Maybe the family scene wasn't for her, but who could argue with a holiday picnic on a sunny day?

"You seem to be having fun," a woman said as she stood over their blanket. She was skylined against the sun, and it took Brady a moment to realize who she was.

She was definitely an unexpected guest at their picnic.

"Mommy," Bella screamed as she jumped up and hugged the woman's legs.

Brady watched as his brother scrambled to his feet. Did Noah have any idea his girlfriend was going to show up in Cape Pursuit?

A cold fist clenched Brady's heart. Was Corrinne there to take her daughter away? He had known Bella staying with them could only be temporary, but he wasn't ready to let her go just yet. Or his brother. What about the house he was hoping to buy? It wouldn't be the same without family to live there with him.

Those thoughts swirled through his head and he knew his concern must have shown on his face because Kate's hand closed over his on the picnic blanket. While Noah hopped up and gave Corrinne a hug and—Brady noticed—a long kiss, Kate leaned close to Brady and whispered, "I'm guessing this is a surprise."

He nodded, unsure what to say as his brother's family had a group hug on their picnic blanket.

"Family surprises are the worst thing about holidays," Kate said with a small grin. "Although I guess it could be the best, too." Despite his worries about the sudden appearance of his brother's girlfriend, he smiled and relaxed for a moment. He hardly knew Corrinne, but he had to trust the fact that having her mother back was the best thing for Bella.

"Maybe I should go," Kate said.

"Don't. Please." Brady had spent the previous Fourth of July holiday alone, and now he had Noah, Bella, Corrinne and Kate. He didn't know how long any of them would be part of his life, but it was good, anyway. Maybe he needed to loosen up on his ideas about stability equaling happiness. Bella and Noah looked pretty darn happy right at that moment.

Brady greeted Corrinne with a friendly hug as soon as Noah and Bella allowed a little space around her, and then he pointed to Kate, who stood on the edge of the blanket as if she was considering escaping the family circle.

"This is my friend, Kate, and this is Bella's mom, Corrinne," he said. He wasn't sure what Corrinne's relationship was with his brother, and Brady wasn't sure his brother knew, either, so calling her Bella's mom seemed like the most accurate and safe description.

"Did you just arrive in Cape Pursuit?" Kate asked as she shook Corrinne's hand. "You picked a busy day."

Corrinne smiled and stroked Bella's hair. "I wasn't expecting the traffic. I've never been here before, and I had been led to believe it was a sleepy beach town. Not party central as it appears to be."

"It's not usually sleepy during the summer, but today is especially crazy because of the holiday," Kate said.

Brady was grateful to Kate for making pleasant small talk, which gave him, Noah and even Bella a chance to absorb the idea of their visitor. What would it mean for all of them?

"Are you hungry?" Noah asked. "I think we cleaned out our picnic basket, but we could get something from one of the food vendors."

Corrinne smiled at Noah, and Brady couldn't help but see her look of pure love for his brother. Were things going to work out for them, after all? For Bella's sake, he hoped so. "I'd love that," she said.

Noah and Corrinne walked toward the food tents with Bella between them holding both their hands. Brady sat back down on the blanket and was relieved when Kate sat next to him, close enough that their legs and elbows touched.

"Okay," Brady said. "And…wow."

Kate laughed. "That's about as speechless as I've ever seen you."

Brady laid back on the blanket and closed his eyes against the sun. "It's been a summer of unexpected moments, so I guess I should toughen up, but I have to say I never expected Corrinne to show up out of the blue."

"She and your brother don't have an official...relationship?"

Brady smiled as he felt Kate lie down next to him. Children, families and even bees buzzed all around them in the sunshine, but he felt as if he was on an island with Kate and somehow she was keeping him afloat despite the major uncertainty he felt about his family's future.

"They used to, and then they had Bella, and then my brother—I think—went through a time when he didn't...well—"

"You don't have to tell me all this," Kate said. "It's none of my business."

Brady wished he knew if she was just being polite or if she really wanted to maintain a layer of disinterest between her affairs and his.

"It's not a secret," he said. "My brother and Corrinne didn't see things the same way when they suddenly found themselves young, unmarried, financially struggling and with a daughter. I tried to help him with extra cash when I could, but that wasn't really fixing the problem."

He felt Kate stir on the blanket next to him and he opened one eye to find her propped on one elbow and staring down at him. "Have you always watched out for your younger brother?"

Brady closed his eyes. "More times than you can imagine. So it was hard to see him struggle."

"You must have been glad when he and Bella came to live with you."

"Ecstatic. And I'll admit I was hoping they would stay. I didn't get a chance to tell you my brother got that job at the bank he interviewed for the day you watched Bella. He's supposed to start work tomorrow." He and Noah had worked out a schedule for at least the next week where they would take turns working, watching Bella and taking her two doors down to a nice older lady who babysat neighborhood kids in the summer.

"That's great," Kate said. "If I know you, you probably already picked out a bedroom for your niece in the houses you've been dreaming about."

Brady smiled but he didn't open his eyes. "The sunniest one in each of them."

"What will happen now?" Kate asked. He felt her shift next to him and he opened his eyes. "Do you think Corrinne will want to stay here, too?"

"I have no idea what she's thinking," Brady admitted. "I did notice she seemed happy to see my brother."

Kate laughed. "That was definitely more than a friendly-hello type of kiss. Maybe wherever she's been has given her some perspective and she realizes she better grab a good guy when she has the chance."

If Kate would apply a fraction of that logic to her own relationship with him, Brady would be the happiest man at the Fourth of July picnic. Had she just admitted that being away from someone might make a person realize what she'd been missing? He touched her cheek with the pads of his fingers, thinking about the times she'd gone away that summer and how she'd seemed happy to see him when she returned. Were her clear lines softening a little?

Brady stretched up and touched a kiss to her lips. Kate returned the kiss, briefly, but then she sat up straighter and glanced around at the park as if she didn't want to be caught kissing him in broad daylight. Did she really care what other people thought, or was she more worried that she'd let her own thoughts get away from her?

"I almost wish I didn't have to go to work in an hour," she said.

"Almost?"

She lifted one shoulder in a little shrug. "I like driving the trolley and racking up hours."

"But?"

"I like being here with you, too," she said, her voice low and meant for him. Brady didn't know how much longer he could hold on to Kate's attention and affection, but he'd be a fool not to enjoy it while it lasted.

CHAPTER SIXTEEN

TWO DAYS LATER, Kate got up early and went for a long walk along the ocean before beginning her morning shift in the office and a fill-in afternoon shift driving the trolley. She'd had a lot of different jobs over the years, and there was always a halfway point where she started to feel a tiny tug of annoyance at the people she worked with, the place where she lived and the job she was doing.

She should be at that point. The summer was slightly more than half over for her, but as she watched the sun rise over the ocean, her thoughts were like the colorful reflections emanating from it. The pastel rays were still beautiful to her, and she wasn't tired of the view. Sure, she would love the view from the window of an airplane wherever her new job would take her. It wouldn't be possible to tire of something that would change nearly every day.

But for the first time, she admitted that she would miss Cape Pursuit. Okay. Second time. If she was being truly honest with herself, she had to confess that there was a reason she had come back for a second season when she had never done a repeat job before. Of course it was the sunrise and the ocean, she assured herself. And there was something very endearing and amusing about the bell on the trolley.

Kate returned to her apartment, showered and put on her uniform and picked up her tablet to check her email. In addition to the usual junk emails, there was a message from the airline school. She laid the tablet on the kitchen counter, took a deep breath and tapped the message to open it.

The first word was *Congratulations*, and Kate leaned on the counter in relief. She hadn't really doubted her chances at admission, but her nomadic lifestyle over the past six years was, in the eyes of some people, a detracting factor. It was hard getting an employment reference when she never stayed in one place for very long. And a permanent address? Also a tough one. She had refused to use her parents' address for the past several years, and she knew that she had been turned down for several jobs because of her unconventional life choices.

But this was a congratulations email. She scanned the rest of the message. It also said she had received a one-thousand-dollar scholarship that was—she recalled—fairly standard for all new entrants. To her surprise, the message also explained another potential one-thousand-dollar scholarship for applicants who were willing to commit to flying internationally for at least one year. An incentive for those who were interested in the long hauls.

Amazing. With potentially double the scholarship amount she had been expecting, Kate was closer to affording school than she'd thought. She could even chop off the last month of her summer job and leave at the beginning of August instead of the beginning of September. She wouldn't need to chase the goal of winning the employee game to be a thousand dollars ahead.

Her first instinct was to wake up Holly and tell her the great news. Kate took one step toward her friend's bedroom door but remembered almost instantly that she was gone. She could call her parents, but her father would be at work and her mother would probably be lukewarm about the news and ask her when she was coming home next.

Brady. He would be happy for her. Would almost certainly give her a big hug and a kiss and tell her how great he thought her news was…even if he didn't necessarily think so. She could picture the light slowly dying in his eyes when he understood that the additional scholarship would mean she would be all over the world with her job and, worse, could leave Cape Pursuit earlier than she had planned.

She shouldn't call him. It was selfish to use him just because she wanted someone to share her great news with, especially when the news might hurt him. But he would know sooner or later, and they were—sort of—dating for the summer, so he should know what her plans were.

Kate's finger hovered over his number, but she decided to text him instead. It would give her time to think about what to say instead of letting the excitement in her voice give her news away.

Dinner tonight? I'm free starting at six and I have some good news to tell you about.

Kate waited. Brady could be at work saving someone or at home making smiley-face pancakes for his niece. After Corrinne had shown up unexpectedly on the Fourth of July, Kate had taken a step back, giving Brady and his family space. Was Corrinne staying at Brady's house with all of them like a big happy family? Would she stay in Cape Pursuit, and what would that mean for Brady?

My shift ends at seven. Meet at my place?

Kate was tempted to say she would rather pick him up and choose the restaurant because this was her idea, her big news, and being the planner also left her in control of the evening. Also, going to Brady's house could be awkward, especially if Corrinne, Noah and Bella were all there. She blew out a breath. He'd said "meet at my place." That didn't mean he would have a romantic table set for two and a photographer on hand to take family photos for the Christmas card.

It was silly to read too much into four little words in a text.

Perfect, she typed into her phone.

Kate lingered over the word before she tapped Send. She used to know what her idea of a perfect day, week and life meant, but her thoughts were getting more and more muddled. Maybe she should leave Cape Pursuit early just to keep her thought-lines clear.

BRADY NEVER MINDED working beyond his scheduled hours. People needed help, and their emergencies were always more important than his planned trips to the grocery store or drive-through burger place. However, he glanced ruefully at his phone as he and Ethan returned to the fire station after taking a patient who had fallen in her home to the hospital. Five minutes past seven. Ever since Kate had texted earlier in the day, he'd been looking forward to seeing her. What was the good news she wanted to share?

On my way, he texted Kate.

Was she sitting in his driveway? He wished he'd had time to mow the lawn and get rid of the dead flowers in the planter on the porch. That red geranium needed more water than a house fire. He'd managed to keep one alive the entire previous summer, but somehow balancing the fire station, the trolley job and his brother and niece had pushed him over the edge into plant-neglect territory.

He would do better when the plants were on his own porch, even if he had to continue working two jobs to make the house payments and have some spare cash for home improvements. Owning his own place was going to be his ticket to happiness, especially if he could provide a home for his brother, too.

Want to reschedule?

Definitely not, Brady texted as Ethan backed the ambulance into the station. Be home in five minutes.

Home. After he sent the message, he wished he had used the word *there* instead. He didn't want Kate to think he was trying to domesticate her and persuade her that his lifestyle was the one for her. He didn't have a right to his rogue thoughts where he pictured her planting flowers in their backyard or hanging up curtains they'd just gone to the home improvement store to choose.

Brady set his truck's cruise control to twenty-five on the side streets just to keep himself from speeding on the way home. When he pulled onto his street and saw Kate's red Escape on the road in front of his house, it looked so right he had to catch his breath. He willed his heart to stop racing. He was home only ten minutes later than planned. As he parked, he saw Kate sitting in the one chair on his concrete front porch.

"Hey," she said, standing as he got out of his truck.

"Sorry I'm late."

She shrugged. "No big deal. Do you need a minute to change before we go out?"

Brady stopped on the top step where he was eye level with Kate. "Would you mind if I order pizza and we eat here?"

It would be intimate and private inviting anyone into his home, but with Kate, he was afraid it was something more: risky. She was clearly not a homebody, and her hesitation at the simple question made him wish he hadn't asked.

"Sure, that's fine," she said.

Before she could change her mind, Brady

unlocked the front door and waited for her to step through first.

"Beer?" he asked.

"Whatever you're having."

He smiled and pulled her into his arms. "I'm having dinner with someone I care about and who reportedly has some good news to share."

"No hurry," Kate said. She tipped her chin up and kissed him lightly. The gesture was friendly and playful, but her eyes were serious. Brady loved the feel of her in his arms, the way her hair brushed his cheek and tickled his neck. Having her in his home added to the poignant sense of time slipping away and the sad knowledge that their dinners, walks on the beach and conversations were finite. He rubbed her back and then let her go so he could hang up his keys and hat and put his wallet in the tray on the table by the front door. His brother's wallet, keys and baseball cap were missing, and Brady knew Noah and Corrinne would be gone a few more hours on their trip with Bella to an amusement park an hour away.

Brady watched Kate as she glanced around his living room. A colorful cardboard dollhouse took up a large space next to the couch, and there were princess DVDs stacked on top of the television. Plastic building blocks were on the coffee table next to a public safety magazine he subscribed to and a pair of his brother's sunglasses. His house wasn't messy, but it wasn't a museum. The personal articles belonging to its occupants were part of what made it a home.

"You probably don't have plastic ponies next to your bathtub and fifteen different hair ribbons in the vanity drawer," Brady said.

"Not now, but I did growing up. I think I had some of those same movies." Kate smiled. "They never go out of style."

Brady felt his shoulders relax. Kate wanted her freedom and had no interest in settling down, but she also never seemed to be judging him for his choices, his life.

"Any special pizza requests?" He got his phone out of his pocket and his finger hovered over the number in his contact list. "I love extra cheese and sausage, but we could always get two smalls or do a half and half."

"I also like extra cheese and sausage, and could we have them put mushrooms on half?"

"We can do the whole. My brother likes

mushrooms, and I've learned to adapt since he's living with me."

Kate cocked her head and he could see a question coming. "Will he stay, now that he seems to be...reunited with Corrinne?"

Brady lowered his phone. "I wish I knew."

"You want him to, and Bella," Kate said. It was more a statement of understanding than a question.

Brady nodded. "It's part of my reason for house shopping. Not all of it, but part."

He wanted to talk about what he suspected was happening with his brother's family, but this evening was about Kate and her news. But first, he was starving. Brady called in his pizza order and then motioned Kate into the kitchen.

"I think the glasses are in that cabinet," he said. "But that could have changed. My brother helps out by emptying the dishwasher, and I'm never quite sure where I'm going to find things."

"You don't have a prearranged place for everything?" Kate asked.

"Do I seem that rigid to you?"

Kate regarded him for a moment. "No, but you do seem organized."

Brady shrugged. "I'm organized about the important things like paying my bills on time, showing up to both my jobs when I'm supposed to and getting my oil changed. But cups and bowls? I don't get too worked up about it."

Kate laughed. "My mother would absolutely lose it if someone moved stuff around in her kitchen."

"Picky?"

"Petrified into a lifetime of habits."

Brady got two beers from the fridge while Kate opened and closed three cabinets before she found two tall clear glasses. She put them on the counter and Brady poured the cold beer into them.

"I thought you were a creature of habit and that's why you want your own house, so you can control the space and keep everything just as you want it," Kate said.

He smiled at her over the edge of his glass before taking a sip. "That's a lot of accusations in one sentence."

"I'm sorry, I didn't mean for it to sound like an accusation."

Brady leaned against the counter. "I want

my own house so I don't wonder where I'm going to be every night."

"But you're renting this place and you don't have to wonder."

He laughed. "Except for sleuthing out where the can opener is, you're right. But it's not the same as having a piece of property to call my own."

Kate sighed. "My parents would love you."

Brady felt his breath catch, and he felt like he'd just opened a window blind in a dark room to find glorious sunshine outside.

Kate sat at the kitchen table and took a drink. She glanced up at Brady, a question on her face, and he realized he was immobilized when he should be sitting down with her. He pulled out a chair and eased into it, almost afraid to break the spell of conversation that might tell him what he wondered about Kate.

"They believe personal property is very important. The house must be just so, the car leased so it's always just a year or two old, furniture tasteful and a patio that looks as if it could be an advertisement for a magazine."

"There's nothing wrong with liking nice things."

"It's wrong to be owned by things."

"Do you think I'll be owned by a house if I manage to get one?"

Kate took a long sip of her beer and didn't meet his eyes. "No," she said quietly.

"So this is why you're always on the move, not wanting to get tied down to anything or anyone."

Anyone like him.

Kate's silence answered the question for her.

"It doesn't have to be that way, Kate. Lots of people have a nice house and a car and a comfortable reclining chair in front of a television, and they keep their perspective."

"I'd rather be out on the open road than behind a television."

Brady clinked his glass against hers. "Which brings us to your big news, which I'm guessing has something to do with flying away."

The words cost him almost as much as the light tone he mustered up to deliver them. If he could keep Kate at his dining room table long enough to convince her he was worth taking a risk, risking her abhorrence of permanent things, risking her heart... Or maybe they could sit there all night and it would never change her mind.

He had to take whatever she was willing to offer, no matter how transitory. The glimmers of happiness were worth it.

She looked at him with a faint smile that told him that he'd managed to turn the tide of their conversation. He couldn't offer her much—she wouldn't take it—but he could offer her an ear and his friendship.

"I got into the flight attendant school and got a big scholarship," she said.

Brady leaned in and kissed her temple. "Congratulations. They're lucky to have you."

If only he were so lucky.

"Thanks. I could double my scholarship if I commit to a year of international flights."

Brady kept his expression the same—at least he hoped so—but his heart sank. He knew she was going away, but as long as he could look up and imagine her crossing over the sky above Cape Pursuit, and as long as the airport only an hour away remained in business, he could keep alive the hope that she might drive into town. Hadn't he been surprised to see her at the beginning of the summer? Maybe she had some surprises left.

"And I'm sure you'll say yes to that," he said, smiling. "What a great opportunity."

The doorbell rang, and Brady got up to get the pizza, but he knew food would never fill up the gaping hole inside him.

CHAPTER SEVENTEEN

"YOU WON," BRADY said as he got on the trolley the next morning to join Kate as her coguide.

"You mean the surfboard, right?" Kate asked from the driver's seat. She had looked at her phone before she got in the shower and was surprised to be the random recipient of the employee prize of a surfboard. She had never owned anything large, other than a car, and her first thought was to wonder where on earth she would stow a surfboard. Could she get a roof rack for the Escape and drive around looking like someone on a permanent vacation?

Brady smiled, but he cocked his head and narrowed his eyes. "You don't seem very enthusiastic for someone who just won a prize valued at around five hundred bucks."

She raised her shoulders and held both hands palms up. "I don't know how to surf, and I don't have any place to keep a surf-board. I'll look pretty silly trying to stuff it into the overhead storage on an airplane as part of my crew luggage."

"You could leave it at my place, but I can't guarantee I won't use it."

"You know how to surf?" Kate didn't know why that surprised her. Brady seemed more like a guy who, by his own admission, liked to keep both feet on the ground. He was un-comfortable with the idea of flying, but he surfed? Maybe she shouldn't try to define him into a neat box.

Brady laughed. "You said that as if I told you I knitted a prize-winning blanket for the county fair last year."

"Did you?"

He shook his head. "Nothing against yarn, but no. But I do like to surf. I'm not likely to win any competitions, but I don't always dis-grace myself, either." He propped a hand on the pole behind her driver's seat. "How about going to the beach after work so you can try out your new board?"

"You want to try it, don't you?" Kate asked.

Brady leaned in and dropped a quick kiss

on her lips. "I want to have fun with you. And maybe your new board. I could teach you."

Kate was not one of those girls who went to summer camp where kids swam in lakes, paddled canoes and climbed trees. Her parents would have considered that a dangerous invitation to scraped knees, leeches and poison ivy. Their family vacations were to carefully controlled and perfectly manicured resorts where, usually, some of her parents' friends or her father's business associates were also vacationing. There had never been surfing or water sports. Instead, there had been five-course dinners and trips to art museums.

"I don't know," she told Brady as she pulled away from the office parking lot. They headed for the first stop where tourists might already be waiting even though it was just eight in the morning.

Brady sat down on the front seat and put his chin on his hands. Kate glanced up at the mirror above her head and saw his dejected-looking reflection. He looked like a boy who wanted a puppy but had been summarily rejected as a pet owner.

"Maybe we could build a sandcastle or

something. I'm afraid I'll humiliate myself trying to surf," she admitted.

"Of course you will," he said. "You'll eat a mouthful of sand as you wash in on your face. I may even have to rescue you. And you'll be too sore tomorrow to even crawl up the steps onto the trolley."

Kate laughed. "So why would I want to do this?"

"Because you of all people aren't afraid to try something new, especially with someone like me as an instructor."

"Someone like you?" she asked.

"Experienced, trustworthy and invested in your survival until at least the end of the summer," Brady said.

Kate was happy to agree to the first two qualities he attributed to himself. The third one gave her heart a little squeeze. She had warned him not to get too involved with her, had never led him to think she'd stick around. He was putting her in an unfair situation.

"And by invested, I mean I'm still hoping to win the top prize and you may be my toughest competition. If I let you die surfing, people will say I'm bumping off the competition," he said with a huge grin she saw reflected in the mirror above her head.

Kate sighed. "Fine. I'll try surfing for a little while, but I have to be able to work tomorrow so I can't take too many chances."

"This is going to be fun," he said.

Later that day, Kate and Brady clocked out after hours of driving tourists to the beach and they headed to the beach themselves. They both went home to change first, and once Kate was in her apartment, she seriously considered chickening out. She had an ocean-blue bathing suit—a one-piece practical garment—that she liked, but she regretted her uneven tan. With fair skin and a lot of time driving the trolley, she was very pale except for tanned forearms and a swath of leg ranging from midthigh where her shorts ended to the sock line at her ankle.

She didn't like looking ridiculous, and she certainly didn't like the feeling of being out of control, which would certainly be part of learning to stand on a narrow board on top of water. Someone else should definitely have won the surfboard prize.

Kate thought about faking a headache or claiming George had called her in to work on some paperwork in the office. Even if Brady suspected it was a ruse, he would smile pleasantly and let her off the hook. But he didn't deserve to be lied to.

She put on the suit, tossed a long T-shirt over it, slid her feet into flip-flops and trudged back to her car. Brady was already waiting at the company office building right next to the beach, and he had her surfboard tucked under his arm. He wore red swim trunks and a white swim shirt.

"I took the liberty of picking up your board for you," he said.

"I'm not sure I'm ready for this," she admitted.

Brady slung his free arm over her shoulders. "You'll love it so much you'll be looking for a way to squeeze this board into your car when you leave town."

Kate tried to imagine the surfboard sticking out of her car as she waved goodbye to Cape Pursuit, but she couldn't complete the image in her mind.

They stopped at the rental shack on the beach and Brady rented a board for one hour. His was a scarred, serviceable-looking board with most of the painted design rubbed off and a chip at one end. The ankle strap was frayed. Kate's new board was shiny and colorful, untested.

Brady laid both boards on the sand near the water's edge. "Just stand on it for a minute," he said. "Get the feel of it while you're on solid ground."

Kate hesitated, unsure how that would help. She already knew how to stand on a nonmoving surface.

"Trust me," Brady encouraged.

Kate stepped onto the board and the added inches brought her height closer to Brady's as he stood right in front of her. She was getting used to the feelings of attraction that wouldn't let go of her when she was with Brady, but the feeling that surprised her as she stood on the board on the beach was that of freedom. Even with Brady standing guard with a steadying hand, she felt weightless and unfettered. Was it the unexpected win of a surfboard that would allow her to glide over the waves, or was it something about having Brady there to catch her if she fell?

She took a deep breath and wished she could put into words what she was feeling, even though it would be far riskier than putting herself at the mercy of the Atlantic Ocean.

"Now or never?" Brady asked. "Let's paddle out."

"And then what?" she asked. Wasn't there going to be more instruction? She couldn't just go out there and start surfing.

"We'll go out and wait," he said. "Surfing takes patience while you keep your eye out for the perfect wave to try to get on top of. I'll tell you everything I know while we're hanging out in water above our heads."

Kate had spent the past six years relying only on herself, but she followed Brady's example, put the ankle strap on her leg and entered the surf right behind him, ready to let go for just a little while.

BRADY BOBBED NEXT to Kate about thirty feet from shore. The waves weren't ideal, and they had to wait in between crests for a good one to attempt. The mid-July evening was hot and humid, but the beach was almost deserted. Most visitors had already had their fill of sun and surf and were showering off in their hotels or going out to enjoy the nightlife of Cape Pursuit. Brady's idea of a perfect evening was exactly like the one he was having—good company and the hope of catching a good wave.

At first, Kate was timid, jumping onto her board and moving a little too late each time. He showed her how to be ready and start paddling.

"How exactly did you learn to surf?" Kate asked.

"From one of my mother's longer-lasting boyfriends when we lived for a summer in Virginia Beach." Things had seemed like they might work out that summer he was fifteen, but when the relationship ended, his idyllic summer did, too. He took a deep breath of ocean air.

"That was ten years ago, but I still remember my first surfing lesson. You're doing great, you just have to let go and trust the water. And yourself."

Brady hopped on and caught two decent waves, riding them onto the beach. Was Kate watching and taking notes? She always seemed confident and in control, so showing her how to enjoy something outside her comfort zone was, he suspected, something not a lot of people experienced. He paddled back to Kate, who was still floating and waiting, and he laid down on his surfboard, relaxing and bobbing with the small waves.

"Are you hoping I'll wear out soon and call it quits?" he asked.

"You only rented that board for an hour, and we have to be getting close."

He laughed. "They can charge me extra when I return it. I want to see you ride at least one good wave before I give up for the evening. You need to prove to yourself you've got it in you."

Her face became grave and he felt he'd crossed over a line suggesting that Kate doubted herself, even though she had jokingly said the same thing. Just as he was afraid he'd ruined a nice evening, she steeled her jaw with pure determination and looked behind her. A decent wave was approaching. Kate kept her eye on it, got on the board and started paddling with it. Brady jumped on his, too, not wanting to be left behind, and paddled alongside Kate.

The wave was larger than it had looked at first, and Brady got to his feet on his board. He risked a glance sideways and found Kate was on her knees and then, precariously but definitely, on her feet. She rode only a few feet before she hit the sand and toppled onto it, but she had done it. Brady was almost sorry she had accomplished the feat because it probably spelled the end of their evening in the fading light and warm ocean.

Brady hopped off his board next to her. "Eat sand?"

Kate laughed. "I had the wisdom to keep my mouth shut. It's a skill I've developed over the years."

"I know a lot of people who could use those kinds of lessons, including myself sometimes."

He pulled both of their boards clear of the water and they sat on them, watching the waves roll gently in and rearrange the sand at the edge of the beach. A white shell drifted in, was sucked out and drifted back again. Brady would happily have sat there all night, just enjoying the companionship and the sweet taste of something fleeting.

"I have to ask you something," he said finally, reluctant to break the spell. "I guess maybe tell you something first, though. My brother's girlfriend had a serious family health issue—heart surgery involving her dad that went well—and it apparently gave her a lot of time to think about what matters."

Corrinne had told him the whole story of the surgery that had come up unexpectedly and how her mother was a wreck and needed Corrinne partly for support and partly to run their family golf course business. Hospital corridors and step-down recovery units are no place for little kids, and it had cost Corrinne a lot to concede she needed help from Noah with their daughter.

"I'm glad her dad is okay," Kate said.

He knew Kate didn't want to get wrapped up in obligations, but when he'd needed her to help him with Bella, she had done it without hesitation. There was a big heart beating in Kate's chest, even if she didn't want the same things he did.

"Anyway," he continued. "With all that thinking, it appears she's decided that it's important for Bella to have a solid family, and she wants to marry my brother and make it official."

"That's great, right?" Kate asked, caution in her voice. "Are you happy about it?"

"Of course I am. I didn't know Corrinne very well before, but she's been living under my roof for two weeks, and I can see how happy she makes Noah. And she's a wonderful mother. No wonder Bella is such a terrific kid."

"It must have been hard for Corrinne leaving Bella with your brother for over a month."

"I'm sure. Just as it would be hard for Noah to be parted from Bella."

And hard for himself. If and when his brother's family got their own place, how would he fill the empty spaces in his home and his heart?

Kate put a hand on his knee. "Are you okay?"

He took a deep breath. "I'm being selfish. It was foolish, but I had this whole plan cooked up where I got a perfect house and my brother and niece moved in with me. Now that Corrinne's back, it reminded me that they should be together and I'm just the lonely uncle."

Kate moved onto his surfboard and put an arm around him. They both watched the water for a few minutes, and Brady enjoyed the comfort Kate offered, just with her presence and for the moment. But it was enough.

"What were you going to ask me?" she finally said.

"Oh." He'd almost forgotten. "The wedding. They want a simple beach wedding and they want to do it soon. Next week."

Kate drew back in surprise. "They're going to put together a wedding in a week?"

Brady shrugged. "They just need time to get a license and for her family to come from West Virginia. Her dad got the okay from his cardiologist to make a short trip. Corrinne's family owns a golf course there, but I guess they're getting someone else to run it while they come down here next weekend."

"Will Noah and Corrinne move to West Virginia after they're married?"

"I don't think so," Brady said. "Noah just started a good job at the bank, and Bella loves the ocean. I haven't asked a lot of questions, but I think they will stay in Cape Pursuit."

"So you won't be so terribly lonely," Kate said, smiling. "Uncle Brady."

"No," he admitted. "But I do still need a date for the wedding."

He saw her hesitate and then flash a quick smile. "Who are you planning to ask?"

Brady laughed. "The girl at the beach shack, as soon as I return this overdue board."

Kate withdrew her arm from around his shoulders and crossed her arms over her chest as she gave him a goofy grin. "I'll make sure we're both marked off on the schedule as soon as you tell me the time and date," she said. "I've never been to a one-week-of-planning wedding, and I think I like the sound of it."

"Have you been to fancy weddings?"

Kate rolled her eyes. "You can't imagine. My parents and their friends believe that weddings are a display of wealth more than affection. You could probably buy a house for the amount my cousins spent on theirs, and a house will sure as heck last longer."

"Was the cake at least good?" Brady asked.

Kate nodded. "And the champagne. It almost dulled my senses enough to ignore my aunts when they demanded to know when my wedding would be."

Brady smiled. "I'm trying to picture you with a cup of expensive champagne."

"Flute," she said. "There are fancy names for all kinds of unnecessary objects, and that's exactly how my family rolls."

"But not you," he said.

"Not true. Look at this pricey surfboard I'm disgracing with my lack of skill. It's just as useless as Waterford crystal, unless I actually learn to operate it."

"You're here for another month, and I think that sounded like a challenge. Or an invitation."

"I might try a few more surfing lessons, but I'll probably have to bequeath this board to you when I leave town," she said, smiling.

Brady tried not to think about her driving away in another month or so, no surfboard sticking out of her Escape, no ties holding her heart.

CHAPTER EIGHTEEN

BRADY SPENT A long night lying awake in his bed. Surfing had tired him physically, but the evening had lit up his senses and ignited a thought that wouldn't go away.

He loved Kate.

He'd never been in love before. Dated some girls in high school, but never seriously. He hadn't gotten close enough for anyone to ask questions about the home life he'd tried to hide. Since then, he'd focused on his firefighting training, career and extra jobs, always with the future goal of a home. A wife and family could come later, but the house had to be first.

There had been a few dates over the years, but Brady wasn't interested in casual transitory relationships. He'd been holding out for the real thing. As he lay looking at the blue numbers on his bedside clock, he had the bitter realization that the two things he wanted most couldn't exist together. He loved Kate, and she had no interest in the kind of permanence he needed like he needed air to breathe.

He was afraid to even ask himself the toughest question. Did Kate love him? He squeezed his eyes shut against the pillow knowing it didn't matter. Even if there was something growing between them, her need to move on and maintain her freedom would overpower it. If he loved her, he had to let her go.

Or—the thought almost jolted him upright in bed—go with her. The thought was pure madness, reckless, even desperate. He had a plan for his life and he was too close to give it up, but…

Kate's future would center around airports, perhaps one airport in particular where she would be based. Didn't airports need firefighters? It would mean giving up the life he'd been building in Cape Pursuit, but he could start fresh somewhere. As he fell asleep, he pictured himself on the ground at an airport, manning the fire station while watching planes come and go all day long. Kate would be on one of those planes, always climbing out of his reach. He didn't remember where his thoughts ended and dreams took over, but in the back of his mind, he couldn't answer the most important question. Did Kate love him, and what would he be willing to risk to find out?

As soon as Brady shut off the alarm and got to the station for an early shift, he already heard the call tones echoing that signaled a fire call. He tossed his backpack into his locker, nodded to Captain Kevin Russell to tell him he was ready for duty even though his shift didn't officially start for another ten minutes. No one punched a clock when people or property were in danger. Brady pulled on his gear and got in the passenger seat of the second pumper where Charlie was already in the driver's seat wearing his turnout gear.

"Were you just about to go home?" Brady asked, knowing he was probably Charlie's replacement.

"Isn't that when fires always happen?" Charlie asked, but his grin erased any cynicism. Brady knew Charlie lived for the rush and also the fulfillment of being a rescuer, just as he did. "My wife will hear it on the scanner and take our baby with her to work, so it's all good."

Brady briefly imagined himself getting home late from work, a wife and kids happy to see him. The wild thought of leaving town and following Kate from the night before made no sense in the daylight. Even if he did quit his job and go with her, would she want him?

"The buyer dropped the price on that blue house you liked," Charlie said. "Hate to take advantage of someone else's misfortune, but they're in a position where they need to unload it fast."

"Really?" Brady said, hope surging in his chest. He adjusted the siren to change its long wail to a quicker warble as they approached an intersection in downtown Cape Pursuit. Charlie hit the brakes and slowed until Brady looked twice and called out a "clear right" from his side of the cab. His thoughts were on the attack plan for the call they were hurrying to, a reported garage fire. The garage was not attached, and the caller said there were no other structures or people in danger, but every fire call was serious, and Brady never let his guard down until they were on the way back to the station.

But that blue house danced before him, enticing him and tempting him to imagine his mismatched dishes in the kitchen cabinets and his ancient push mower in the garage.

"We'll talk about it later," Brady said. "Any idea if there are hazardous materials stored in this garage?"

Charlie let out a short humorless laugh. "It's a garage. You know there will be a gas can, a bucket of something that looks like used motor oil, lawn chemicals and fifteen cans of half-empty spray paint."

Brady smiled. "Nice to know you can count on some things."

They were the second fire truck to leave the station, and the first one was already blocking the street in front of the burning structure. Gavin and Kevin had the hydrant hooked and were rolling out long stretches of hoses. Charlie stopped the truck, Brady hopped out and chocked the wheels and they reported to Kevin for orders.

It didn't take long to knock down the fire in the small structure, and when the fire was out, Kevin and Brady worked together to stack the fire hoses back on the truck while Charlie and Gavin picked up equipment. It was hot, and Brady put his helmet and coat in the cab of the truck leaving on his sweaty T-shirt, bunker pants and heavy boots.

"You ever think about your future?" Kevin said as he waited in the hose bed for Brady to hand up hose.

Brady's attention caught at Kevin's serious tone. Was he in trouble for something? Kevin was a captain and a cousin of the chief. Was there something Brady needed to know?

"My immediate future," Brady said, trying for a cheerful tone, "involves a shower and a sandwich."

Kevin laughed. "Mine, too. But I mean on the department. We're always on the look-out for good officers, and you've put in five years now."

An officer. Brady respected and admired the leaders on the department, and it always seemed like a someday goal for him. As soon as he got established, bought a house, had a permanent address…then he could think about furthering his career. When he didn't have to work two jobs anymore to save for a down payment, he would have time to go to evening or weekend classes at the State Fire Academy.

"It's something I've always wanted," he said.

"Good. Tony will probably put out a call soon for anyone interested in classes, and I know he's got you on the top of his list."

"Thanks." Brady felt a glow in his chest. He'd come a long way from being practically homeless as a child to being a man entrusted with saving people and possibly even becoming a leader. And being an officer came with a small but decent raise—extra money that would come in handy if his house needed plumbing work or a new swing for the porch. He pictured himself coming home to that perfect blue house.

On the way back to the station, Charlie fanned the flames even more by talking about how he should jump on that house before someone else did, how property values were going up in that neighborhood, how it was a perfect time of year to close on a deal and be ready to rake the fall leaves.

Call me, Brady texted to his brother, knowing Noah would check his phone at lunch. He didn't want to pressure his brother about his future housing plans, especially with a wedding in just a week, but he had to share the amazing news with someone. Noah, more than anyone, would understand what a home meant to Brady and what being offered a chance at advancement on the fire department would mean.

He could text Kate, but he knew she would also be busy working. She'd be happy for him in a friend-cheering-on-a-friend way, but she wouldn't understand. To her, a home meant confinement. To him, it meant freedom from uncertainty, want and even fear. A person who had grown up like Kate wouldn't see it that way, no matter how much he wished he could explain.

"DO YOU HAVE a few minutes?" George asked as Kate punched out after her dayshift driving the trolley.

"Sure," she said. She didn't have to check her watch. She knew it was just past four, and even though she was planning to take advantage of the Friday night tourist crowd by driving for Uber, she could spare a moment for George. The guy was overworked and seemed anxious lately, but Kate also admired the way he'd tried to build an employee culture throughout the summer. He didn't have to do that. He could have just paid minimum wage and hoped some of them would return for the next season out of loyalty to a pay-check if nothing else.

He gestured for Kate to come into his office and pointed to a chair across from his desk. The surface of the desk held a computer, piles of papers, a stapler, a paperweight with a seashell embedded in its glass surface, two plastic drink cups from fast-food restaurants and a faded blue hat with an older Cape Pursuit Trolley logo. Kate knew he spent a lot of time there, but his desk suggested he'd been living there for ten years.

"I actually used the surfboard already," she said as she sat in a red plastic chair that was missing one foot and teetered when she moved.

He looked up, a question on his face. "Oh, that's right. You won it. I hope you had fun."

Kate laughed. "Learning to surf is more challenging than fun, but I'm willing to give it another try. Brady went with me."

She didn't know why she added that fact. Of course a lot of people knew she was dating Brady; it wasn't something they'd kept secret or hidden. There was no reason to conceal something that was uncomplicated and shared the same timeline their summer jobs did.

"He's a good guy," George commented, but he seemed distracted.

"Is there something I can help you with?"

"I hope so. You've probably noticed that this summer has been…different from last summer. I've tried some new things, attempted some organization and reorganization."

Kate kept a neutral expression as she looked at his desk, a not-so-stellar example of his organization.

"I know," he said, smiling. "I said I attempted it. What I really need is good help. Full-time help. Someone to be my business manager."

He stared at Kate as he spoke, and she had the sinking feeling that the potential business manager wore a nametag that said *Kate* in George's mind.

She cleared her throat. "That's a good idea. Every business needs someone to keep order and keep the books."

"I was hoping you'd think so," he said. "I want to let you in on something that's been going on in my mind for a while and it's happening now." He paused and tapped a pen on his desk. "I'm buying out one of the other summer tourist outfits—Cape Suntimes. They do some shuttles and tours, run two food stands and three souvenir places."

"Wow," Kate said. "I didn't know they were selling. I've seen their coupon booklets all over town." Kate had a few acquaintances who worked for the competing company, and she'd been to their souvenir shops and food stands many times. She'd even taken one of their evening ghost tours of Cape Pursuit. It was sort of a shame to see the company sell out, even though she liked George and knew he'd do a good job. It was just that if and when she returned to Cape Pursuit sometime in the future, maybe some summer for a visit, it wouldn't be quite the same.

Not that she planned to come back, of course. But there was something about the town that it had begun to feel like her home base in all her wandering. Like a place she might come back to for an anchor when she needed one.

"They've been talking about selling," George said. "They're getting older, and their kids aren't interested. And let's face it, there's a lot of competition in this town so getting more of the tourist trade under one umbrella is a smart move for me."

Kate nodded and waited for him to go on. She wondered if Brady knew any of this already. She wouldn't be surprised if he knew the owners of Cape Suntimes.

"So," he said. "I really need a person to be my chief operating officer. Someone who knows my business and has good relationships with other people in town. Someone I already trust and value. What do you say, Kate?"

Of course she would say no. She had her acceptance letter and scholarship offer, her portal to a new career that would be everything she wanted in a job. There was no question of tying herself down to Cape Pursuit and sifting through the mountain of paperwork included in the job. But she was stuck on something else George had said. She had good relationships with people in Cape Pursuit? Was that his perception of her? If so, he wasn't paying attention and apparently didn't know that she, of all people, kept her emotional baggage packed and neatly waiting by the door. She didn't move in and didn't get comfortable anywhere. Certainly not long enough to become territorial and begin thinking about buying luxury sheets and tickets to the local symphony.

"Sorry," she said slowly, turning the small word into a drawn-out one. "I'm happy and excited for you, but I thought you knew I didn't plan to stay in Cape Pursuit."

"You didn't plan to come back this year, but you did," he said.

"It—it's a good job," Kate stammered, knowing it was only part of the reason.

"And I thought you might have changed your mind now that you're dating someone here, and…"

She hardly heard the end of his sentence. Assumptions. That was what drove her away from home. *When are you getting married? Maybe you should get a nicer car, and did you hear that our neighbors are installing a putting green in their backyard?*

"Nothing has changed," she said, her words falling like ice cubes into an empty glass. Did he really think she would alter her plans just because of a summer…flirtation, friendship, *romance*?

She could and would walk away from Brady anytime.

"Maybe a trial run?" George asked. "You could help me with the transition and find someone to hire full-time. Could you give me a month while I get my feet under me?"

Kate rose to her feet. "I'm sorry, George. I have to leave September first, and I can't change my plans. You would be better off finding someone permanent right now and save yourself the trouble of training someone twice."

"But you already—"

"I have to go," she said. "Thank you for the offer, but I can't take it."

Kate needed air. Two ideas warred in her head, and she knew she had to get away from the stuffy cluttered office before her oxygen ran out. She'd like to help George, who was a good guy and had treated her and the other summer workers well. But that wasn't the main reason she was tempted by his offer. There had been the briefest of moments when she'd considered the benefit of staying in Cape Pursuit and the thought of Brady's happy reaction flitted over the floor of her mind.

That was a dangerous thought. Even if she admitted to him that her heart was getting entangled with his, she didn't know what was in his thoughts. She wasn't going to toss away her plans on a maybe-romance that had no future. Staying one more month could lead to another, and she would be leading herself down a path going the wrong direction. She deserved to follow her own dream.

CHAPTER NINETEEN

BRADY PICKED UP Kate the following Sunday afternoon. His suit jacket confined his shoulders, and his collar chafed, but all thoughts of discomfort went out the window when he saw Kate. She wore a blue dress that enhanced the ocean blue of her eyes, high-heeled shoes, a glittering necklace that showed off her beautiful neck and her hair was long and loose.

He was happy for his brother, but he wished he was taking Kate somewhere special where they could be alone instead of attending a hastily planned wedding on the boardwalk and a reception in the party room of a beachfront restaurant. Kate deserved a party and evening all for herself.

"You'll outshine the bride," he said as he hopped out and opened the side door of his truck for her. He'd carefully hand-washed the truck in his driveway and tried to ignore the small spots of rust breaking through the dark gray paint. The vehicle would have to last at least another five years because he hoped to pour his present and future earnings into a home instead.

"Impossible," Kate said. "And not recommended. I've been to plenty of weddings, and it's practically a felony to try to garner more attention than the bride. It's her day."

Brady paused a moment before closing Kate's door, long enough to lean in for a quick kiss.

Kate smiled as she pulled back from the kiss. "You seem nervous."

"I just want to do my part correctly. This should be the happiest day of Noah's life, and I want to help make sure that's what it is."

Brady went around the truck and got in the driver's seat, his heart heavy from the phone call he'd received from his aunt in Florida the day before. His expectations were low, but it was still disappointing.

"I'll be his only family there," Brady said as he pulled out into the weekend traffic. "My mother was invited, but she's not able to come."

"Short notice," Kate said, her words a suggestion.

Brady swallowed and nodded. "That's part of it. And her health…it isn't the greatest."

That was also part of it, but not the entire truth. His mother didn't own a car and lived with her sister in a Tampa trailer park. The two sisters got along well, and he believed his mother's needs were met, but his aunt's charity apparently didn't extend to driving the mother of the groom to an out of state wedding with only a week's notice.

"Sorry to hear that," Kate said.

"It could be for the best," Brady said. "It's been a while since we've seen her."

He had offered her a home with him when he got his full-time firefighting job and a rental house, but she had declined saying she was staying put for the first time in her life. Done moving around, was how she'd put it. Because he could sympathize with that sentiment probably better than anyone else on earth, he hadn't pushed it and, he had to admit to himself, it was a relief. He loved and cared about his mother, but their relationship had been far from the norm.

"I'm sure you have a wonderful speech prepared, and I can't wait to see Corrinne's and Bella's dresses."

Brady gave her a quick grin. "You care about dresses?"

"Of course I do. Just because I don't want to join my parents' country club and have the challenge of choosing the right cocktail dress for each night of the week doesn't mean I don't like dressing up once in a while. This blue one I'm wearing has traveled with me thousands of miles even though it seldom makes it out of my suitcase."

"It should," Brady said.

"Thank you," Kate said, laughing. "I'm glad it has tonight. I'm excited about a casual beach wedding, and I'm fully prepared to take my shoes off if necessary."

Brady turned into the beach parking lot, which was only half-full. Some tourists were still on the beach, and the rest of the cars were Corrinne's family, who had driven down. Seeing at least six cars with West Virginia license plates reminded him how little he and Noah had to offer in terms of family, but how important they were to each other.

Was he losing his brother to Corrinne's family? Brady had asked Noah directly where he planned to live after the wedding, and Noah had said he planned to stay in

Cape Pursuit at least for a while until they got on their feet financially. After that, Noah couldn't make any promises.

"Are you okay?" Kate said. "I've only seen a few flashes of your trademark smile, and this is a happy occasion."

Brady turned off the engine and reached for Kate's hand. "Sorry," he said. "I've always tried to pave the way for my brother, but he's going down a road now I haven't traveled."

Kate laughed. "He's not plunging off a cliff, and he's an adult."

"You're right. I need to relax and enjoy the evening."

He knew he wasn't telling her the whole story, but what did it matter? She would be gone in a matter of weeks, and he would be left to sort out his life and his feelings.

"That's the spirit," Kate said. "And if there's dancing at the reception, I promise I'll save all of mine for you."

Brady smiled. "That thought just might help me survive the ceremony, twelve hundred pictures and my official best man toast."

"I won't let you down."

Brady leaned over and pressed a kiss to her lips instead of searching for any words.

IF BRADY WERE anyone else, she would have entertained him over dinner or while they waited for the cake cutting with the story of George asking her to be his full-time business manager. However, sharing that information with Brady would be as cruel as showing someone their heart's desire and then explaining why they can't have it.

"Bella is behaving like a champion flower girl," Kate said. The little girl, in a white dress that shared a matching red ribbon with her mother's white dress, sat on her grandmother's lap at the head table. The party room at the restaurant was just large enough for several long tables with guest seating, a buffet table and a small dance floor. The decor was simple and elegant, and there were candles on the tables. A two-tiered wedding cake had its own round table, and Kate was relieved when the bride and groom used silver forks to carefully feed each other the ceremonial first slice instead of doing the cake-smearing some people chose to do.

I sound like my mother, she thought as she watched the bride neatly dab at her lips.

"She's a little angel," Brady said. "Except on her bike, then she's more of a daredevil."

"I'm sure you're glad she'll be staying in Cape Pursuit for a while."

Brady nodded. "I don't have much family, so I really appreciate the ones I have."

Kate felt his words as if they were a slap. Did he think she didn't appreciate her family? Sure, she didn't care to visit them often, and she didn't want a lifestyle anything like theirs. She disapproved of their materialism and their focus on the way everything had to look...but she appreciated them...didn't she?

"Ready for that dance?" Brady asked.

Kate's cheeks felt hot. "In a minute. I'm just going to the ladies' room first."

Without waiting for a response, she turned and left the party room, heading for a long hallway with a red exit sign at the end. Maybe it led to the restrooms, and maybe it just led outside. Either one would work.

What was she doing, getting mixed up with Brady and his family—and letting her own feelings get mixed up? She had depended entirely upon her own instincts for six years. It was no time to start looking for approval from someone now.

She saw the ladies' sign and shoved through the door, hoping for a moment of solitude to pull herself together. She dispensed a wad of paper towel and ran it under the cold water, and then she pressed it to her face and neck. "This is why I stay unattached," she reminded her reflection.

It was true. When you loved someone, they felt they had the right to impose their beliefs on you. Could make you feel bad about your choices or try to influence them. She felt the weight lift from her shoulders when she closed her eyes and pictured herself taking off in an airplane, headed for someplace new every day.

"Kate."

She heard Brady's voice outside the restroom door. He knocked and then knocked again. Had he really pursued her to the bathroom? She should have taken the exit instead. This was getting out of hand.

"I have to go," he said. "And I need your help."

There was something in his voice that made her toss her paper towel in the trash and fling open the door.

Brady held his phone up. "Missing person. All hands."

"But it's your brother's wedding," Kate said.

He nodded. "It's all over but the dancing, and the only person I'm disappointing by leaving is you."

She almost told him she wasn't disappointed to miss out on a dance with him, but her heart told her those words wouldn't ring true. Hadn't she just thought about her impossible love for him as she stared in the mirror? If she didn't care about him, she wouldn't be sponging her face with cold water in the bathroom.

"Do you need help?" she asked.

"With the search? We need all the help we can get. The police department is organizing its citizen auxiliary search team, but it's going to be a long night. The missing man is elderly, diabetic, possibly with dementia. Every minute matters."

"I know every street in town after my two driving jobs this summer," Kate said. "Let's go."

She gave a thought to her dress and high heels, but then she decided that action was more important than comfort. Part of her felt guilty for being glad for a distraction, a reason to leave the wedding where so many feelings crowded in on her.

Brady drove them to the police station where an officer was dividing up volunteers. Brady leaned in. "Much as I hate it, would you mind splitting up? We need a strong person leading each group, and you've got more sense and knowledge than most people I know."

She told herself that the only opinion about herself that mattered was her own, but Brady's words warmed her thoroughly despite the cool evening air on her bare arms and legs. Kate got her instructions from the police officer. They included a picture of the missing man, his name and a contact phone number if they found anything. He was a tourist, there with his family in a rental house, and he wouldn't know the way home.

"Here's a radio so you can follow the traffic but be careful what you say over the air. Stay on channel five," the officer said as he pressed a small black radio into Kate's hand. In her years of driving, she had become comfortable using a radio, chatting with other drivers sometimes, once or twice using it to contact police and alert them about an accident or a road hazard.

This felt more personal. She and her group

were tasked with searching a neighborhood that was bordered by the beach on one side and part of a downtown street on the other. The missing man's vacation home was several blocks over, but the groups were using a grid pattern to cover as much of the city as possible.

Kate glanced over at Brady who waved at her with his radio and sent her an encouraging smile.

"What do we do if we find him?" an older woman in Kate's small group asked.

"We do our best to make sure he's okay and we call it in," Kate said.

She led her group to their appointed location. In addition to the older woman, there was a man who identified himself as a volunteer firefighter from Indiana who was there on vacation and joined the search. He had two teenagers with him who looked eager to help and carried flashlights.

"Here is the cross street marking the edge of our grid section," Kate said. "Let's try to stay within sight of each other and regroup at every intersection as we move that way." She pointed and started walking, picking her way in her impractical heels. Should she have asked Brady to take her home so she could change? She didn't want to waste any time. If the man didn't have his medication and was lost for hours, she feared what could happen to him.

Kate thought of her own grandparents. They lived twenty minutes away from her parents and belonged to the same social world. Her grandmother had a standing appointment once a week to have her hair done, and her grandfather had a weekly tee time at the club. They lived according to a schedule and carefully constructed rules, and the last time Kate had seen them was at her cousin Lillie's wedding a year ago. Her grandparents had tried to "talk some sense into her," as they put it. They wanted her to put her energy into their charity, and they tried to give her their four-year-old Mercedes as a gift.

Kate didn't want to be bound to their world, but she also felt a cold slice of fear when she imagined them missing, in need of medication or a meal. She would hike over a mountain in her high heels if it was someone she loved, no matter how far apart they seemed sometimes.

Almost an hour of searching doorways,

benches, darkened side streets and stretches of beach went by, and Kate felt a blister burning the heel of one foot and her little toe on the other.

"We found him," a voice said over the radio. Kate recognized Brady's voice as if he was standing right behind her. "Corner of Ocean and Williams."

"Roger," another voice said over the radio. "Advise if a squad is needed."

"As a precaution, yes," Brady said.

The fear and panic Kate had felt for the missing man and his anxious family dissolved at the sound of Brady's words. Brady would take care of the man and make sure he was all right. The feeling of security that washed over her made her tired knees weak, and Kate wished Brady's protective arms were around her.

I just need two Band-Aids for my feet, she thought, not wanting to read too much into her reaction as she rounded up her small team and shared the good news. They began walking back toward the police station, and with each step Kate faced something she had been unwilling to see all summer long.

Being in one place and connecting her

heart with another person didn't have to be a trap. It could also be a source of strength that would let her soar. Was it possible, somehow, to become a flight attendant but establish a home base nearby? There were airports within an hour; Norfolk was even closer. She tried to imagine coming home to Brady after a long day of flying around the world. There was only one way it could work—if Brady loved her enough and she was willing to take the greatest risk of her life.

She quickened her steps, anxious to see Brady at the end of the search and perhaps even give him a glimpse of her feelings. Maybe it was the emotions of the wedding and the search party, but she felt vulnerable and willing to take a risk.

Kate and her team came across Brady and the elderly man on the way back to the station, and she saw Brady step into the back of an ambulance. Even from a distance, she knew him for his broad shoulders and dark hair, and also the fact that he was wearing a suit. Was he going to the hospital with the man?

A small crowd of family members stayed behind as the ambulance pulled away, and

Kate had to avert her eyes. They stood together, their arms around each other and their shoulders shaking as they cried together. Their relief mixed with joy hit Kate's vulnerable emotions like a truck, and she said a hasty good night to her group before turning to walk home.

She'd almost told Brady that giving her heart to someone and someplace was worth the risk, but seeing the emotionally exhausted family members of the elderly man reminded her why she was probably better off if she kept her hands on the steering wheel and her view pointed to the horizon. With great love and security also came the risk of losing it all. Maintaining her freedom meant a life free of painful heartaches.

CHAPTER TWENTY

"I'M NOT USUALLY on this end of the fire," Brady said as he lit a pile of logs on the beach near the trolley company's office.

"That's why I thought you were the perfect man for the job," Kate said. "It's good to get out of your comfort zone. That's what you told me when you made me go surfing."

Brady added some kindling sticks and coaxed the flame as he knelt in the sand. He looked up at Kate, who stood over him with a to-do list in her hand. "I like my comfort zone," he said.

Kate nodded, and Brady wished for the hundredth time that summer that she would let down her guard and let him in. It was already the second week of August, and he knew the inevitable end of the season was approaching. Everything seemed to be changing rapidly, and Brady felt the same frightening insecurity that had made up most of his childhood. The shifting sand under his knees was a metaphor for his life, and he was tired of it.

"Hey," Kate said softly, putting a hand on his shoulder. "This is supposed to be a party, but you seem so serious tonight."

Brady reached up and put a hand over hers as it lay on his shoulder. Only hours earlier, Noah had told him that he planned to get a house of his own in Cape Pursuit. His new wife's family had offered financial help, and Noah had already contacted a Realtor in town. Brady's heart had sunk as he realized he would be alone again in his own house, alone in his plan to buy something permanent and provide for Noah.

Noah didn't need him now. In fact, his younger brother, whom he had always looked out for, was suddenly getting all the things Brady wanted for himself. Noah had a wife, a beautiful daughter and would soon have a home.

Brady bent back down to fan the flame and arrange the sticks, unwilling to let Kate see his face. He wasn't jealous; it wasn't something ugly like that. It was more a feeling of being…adrift. No one needed him, and that realization left him with the blank slate of his own feelings. What did he want?

"The caterers are here," Kate said as she walked over to them across the sand. Brady sat back on his heels and watched the small fire grow. In less than an hour, the other summer employees from the Cape Pursuit Trolley Company would arrive for a beach party complete with food and a live band, and for the first time, they would be joined by the employees from the new company George was acquiring in a bold business move.

It seemed everyone was reaching for their dreams. Brady glanced over to Kate and watched her talking animatedly with the caterers and then helping them carry tables and cooking equipment to a setup on the beach.

It was a mistake to tie his dream to one person. He'd watched his mother chase the elusive happy ending with one guy after another, and it had nearly destroyed her. She'd kept hoping the next boyfriend would be the one… but he never was. Brady couldn't allow himself to go down that road and pour his heart into chasing something he couldn't have.

Kate had already said no, as often and as nicely as she could. His brother had found his own happiness. Brady took his eyes from Kate and turned to watch the waves rolling in on the beach. Cape Pursuit was his home now. It wouldn't be easy to afford the blue house without his brother's income, too. It wouldn't be the same living there by himself with no playset in the backyard for Bella. But he owed it to himself to buy the house and settle in, anyway, even if he was by himself.

KATE HAD TWO weeks left in Cape Pursuit. The beach bonfire almost felt like a going-away party for many of the summer employees who would soon go back to high school or college as the summer wound down. The weather was perfect, the food smelled great and there were so many employees from both George's old and new companies that it was impossible to be lonely in such a crowd.

Brady still looked lonely. Kate was busy managing and organizing the party as a favor to George as his very temporary and part-time office helper, but she still kept an eye on Brady as he drifted from group to group. She watched him pick at a plate of food before tossing half of it into a trash can. He smiled and talked with some of the other summer workers, probably joking about the silly things that always happened when tourists, sunshine and alcohol mixed.

But he still seemed apart from everyone else. Maybe it was because most of the summer workers were moving on to something else at the end of the season, but he was staying put, right there in Cape Pursuit where he would continue saving lives and taking care of other people.

Kate checked on the caterers, who were transitioning from barbecue food to s'more offerings, made sure the band members had fresh bottles of water and helped hand out marshmallow roasting sticks.

"You haven't stopped working for almost two hours," Brady said as he appeared by her side with an orange soda, which he held out for her. "Take a short break or you'll be worn out before the flames subside."

"Have you been feeding the fire?" Kate asked.

He shook his head. "Not in a while. We want it to burn down low for roasting marshmallows, and I can't leave until I'm sure it's no threat."

Kate wanted to ask if he was in a hurry to

leave, but she was afraid she already knew the answer to that question. Brady, with his usual ready laugh and smile, didn't seem as if he was having fun tonight. He was a few years older than the other summer workers; maybe that was it. Or maybe it was because instead of raking in summer cash so he could get out of town and go off to college or adventures, he was saving money so he could stay right there. It was a big difference.

"I doubt a beach fire is likely to spread," Kate said.

Brady glanced over at the party scene on the beach. "Any time you play with fire, it's dangerous."

Kate was sure there was more to his words, but what could she say? She had tried hard all summer not to burn Brady. She'd been truthful. How could she help it if he had a different plan for his life? Her hand around the bottle of soda was freezing, but she didn't want to take a drink. The lump in her throat would choke her, and she felt frustrated and out of things to say.

The music from the band stopped, and she heard her boss on the microphone asking everyone to approach the makeshift stage for some announcements. Kate knew what was coming because she'd helped him write his remarks and make sure he didn't forget to thank anyone.

"I have to go help," she said. Brady nodded and forced a smile, and Kate felt him behind her as she walked over to the stage. She put her bottle of soda, Brady's sweet offering, on the edge of the stage platform so she would have her hands free to applaud George's announcements and remarks.

A circle of nearly fifty people stood around, some of them still eating finger food from plates or sipping soda, as George talked about the partnership of his own company and the new one he had purchased. He welcomed all the new employees under his umbrella and talked about his excitement about moving forward and providing the best tourist experience for visitors to Cape Pursuit.

It was all exactly as she and George had scripted.

"And now I have to thank the person who made tonight possible by organizing it all," he said, turning to Kate and pointing to her. Even though his words had not been part of the script, Kate gave a smile and little wave to the crowd to acknowledge their polite applause. Brady had faded back into the summer workers, and she was alone. Being alone was nothing new for her. Ever since she'd left home and pursued her own way across the country and back, Kate had been comfortable in her own skin and calling her own shots.

But she still wished Brady hadn't stepped quite so far back into the crowd.

"Kate has been invaluable to me this summer," George continued, and Kate felt her empty stomach clench as she wished he would stop talking and drawing attention to her. "She's a second-year employee, and I was darn glad to see her back this year. I hope all of you choose to come back next year, too, and become part of the Cape Pursuit family. But Kate didn't just drive the trolley for me this year. She stepped up when I needed office help, she was there when another one of our workers needed some help and she even joined the rescue effort for a missing person in town last week."

Please stop talking, Kate thought. He was trying to make her sound like some kind of a hero, but she wasn't. The real hero had disappeared so far back into the crowd that she couldn't even see him.

"You can imagine how disappointed I was when I offered the full-time manager's role to Kate and asked her to stay on permanently and she turned me down." George pointed to Kate with the microphone. "I wish you luck, but I sure wish you'd change your mind and stay."

Kate smiled and shook her head, hoping George would move on to the prearranged list of people he was supposed to thank. Kate risked a glance into the crowd to find Brady, but she only saw his back as he walked across the sand toward the parking lot. She'd never told him she was offered a good job right there in Cape Pursuit. There hadn't been any point, and it wouldn't have changed anything.

Still, she wished he had heard that from her instead of being blindsided with the information at the beach party.

CHAPTER TWENTY-ONE

THE FIREFIGHTERS AT Cape Pursuit didn't usually celebrate birthdays unless it was a milestone one that gave them the opportunity to razz someone over turning forty or even fifty. However, Brady's new sister-in-law had stopped by the station with Bella and a sheet cake that said *Happy 25th Birthday, Brady,* and he was never going to live it down.

"It's your turn to cook tonight," Tony said, "but you could buy us pizza instead since it's your birthday and all."

Brady laughed and took a paper plate with a slice of the cake on it.

"I picked out the cake," Bella said.

"Nice job," Brady said. "It's perfect, honey. Thank you."

Corrinne handed him a plastic fork from the box she'd brought. "You should be glad it didn't have a princess or a pirate on it. I talked her into the one with just balloons and hearts."

Brady smiled at his new sister-in-law. Corrinne seemed happy and content, and ready to put down roots there as a family. His brother had gone from a precarious relationship built around co-parenting Bella to marriage and a solid future in less than one summer. Brady's summer had been eventful, but his brother had upstaged him completely.

"We can't stay," Corrinne said. "We don't want to be in the way, and we're meeting Noah during his lunch to look at a house."

Brady nodded. His brother was wasting no time trying to find a home for his family. Brady had done everything he could to make his home welcoming and encourage his brother to stay as long as he wanted to, but he understood his brother's decision. It's probably what he would do, too, and that's why he'd given Noah the list of houses that were affordable but nice. Most of them Brady had already looked at himself, so he shared all the inside information with Noah and Corrinne to make their search easier.

"Thanks for bringing cake for the department. They'll give me all kinds of crap about it, but that won't stop them from eating the whole thing before the evening shift gets here."

As Brady inspected trucks and worked on a troublesome backup pump on the rescue truck, he thought about what it meant to be twenty-five. He knew his parents had met while they were young, so his father—whoever and wherever he was—probably had two children by the time he was a quarter century old. What would it have been like to grow up with both parents in one house? Would he and Noah have such a tight bond, and would Brady have become a rescuer if he'd enjoyed an idyllic childhood?

He would never know. What he did know was that each year was getting better. A home and a career advancement were within sight, and his feet were on solid ground—except for his relationship with Kate, which was, at best, up in the air.

Brady and two other firefighters got called out on a small fire that they quickly quenched. It was a grass fire at a campground outside of town that grew out of an unattended campfire. It was immensely satisfying to put out the fire, talk with some kids who gawked at the fire trucks and go home knowing he'd done something useful. It was even better than blowing out birthday candles, even though he hadn't paused to make a wish first. As dinnertime approached, Brady took Tony's suggestion and ordered pizzas for the five guys on duty. When he went outside to meet the pizza delivery car in front of the station, he was surprised to see Kate driving slowly past. When she saw him, she pulled into the small lot next to the station. What was she doing there?

Brady paid for the two large pizzas and handed them off to Gavin inside the station, and then he went back outside to meet Kate. She still wore her trolley uniform, and her hair was pulled back in a ponytail. He'd thought her attractive the previous summer, but his feelings for her had gone far beyond appreciating her pretty face and lovely eyes. Every hour he'd spent with her over the summer had deepened his wish that she would stay, even though she seemed to him like a beautiful butterfly with delicate but determined wings.

"Happy birthday," she said as she stopped in front of him. She didn't greet him with a kiss, but she put her arms around his neck for a quick hug. "It's the big twenty-five, isn't it?"

"How did you know?" he said, wishing the hug lasted longer after he felt her pulling away. "Did my brother or Corrinne tell you?"

She shook her head. "I noticed it on your employee ID when I scanned it earlier this summer."

"You have a good memory." He recalled that day when they'd met in the break room. Their relationship had seemed full of mystery and possibility at the time, and how much had it changed?

"Too good," Kate said. "If you remember everything you've done and all the things that make up your past, it's more of a temptation to dwell on them. That's why I prefer to think about the future where I haven't made any mistakes yet."

Brady waited, unsure what to say or what to make of her surprise visit. He hadn't talked to her since two nights earlier when he'd heard George announce that Kate had turned down a great opportunity to stay in Cape Pursuit. Brady was ashamed of his own cowardly behavior in choosing to leave after that announcement instead of sticking around and spending time with Kate. She'd been presented with a clear and easy way of staying, a job that she would probably enjoy, and she'd turned it down. She hadn't even told him about it herself…and why not? Was she afraid he would have tried to persuade her to take the job? She needn't have worried. He'd stuck to the rules all summer, no matter how much it hurt.

"Anyway," Kate said. "I had an hour's break between my regular shift and an evening one I picked up, and I just wanted to say hello and I hope you're having a good day even though you have to work."

"I love my work, so I don't mind being on duty on my birthday. And I didn't have any plans, anyway."

Kate's expression sobered, and he thought he saw her eyes shining as if there were tears in them. He had never seen her cry, and he sure didn't want to be the cause of it.

"I haven't done a very good job of this," Kate said. "Being a summer romance."

It was almost the last thing he thought she was going to say.

"It's not a job," he said. "Not an obligation or something you have to do or even succeed at. You don't owe me anything, Kate. There was never a contract even though we both knew there was an expiration date."

"I'm sorry," she said.

"Why?" Seeing her pained expression, Brady suddenly felt something shift. He reached out and touched a hand to her cheek. "You know what? This has been the best summer of my life. I got to see my brother get married and be happy. They're getting a house of their own now, and I hope they'll live close by. I'm really close to buying my own place. And I'm in line for officer training and a promotion here."

Kate smiled and her expression lightened a bit. "That's quite a list of good things."

"And you're on that list, too," Brady said. "At the top." He realized he had nothing to lose by going one giant step farther and saying what was really in his heart. "You know, twenty-five seems like one of those turning points in a person's life where you think someone might have it all figured out."

"It sounds like you do," Kate said. "You're the most put-together person I know. Your goals are clear, you know what will make you happy and the tourists all think you're the best trolley driver. I've seen the comment cards."

Brady laughed.

"So you see why I say you've got it all figured out, far better than most people," Kate added.

"I think I may have more questions than answers right now, and I don't think it's because I just got a year older." He paused and rolled his shoulders, trying to think through his words before he said them. "I thought it was a sad thing that my brother didn't want or need to live with me anymore, now that he's married. I panicked for a minute when I realized I don't need to watch out for him anymore. I wasted some regret on that the past few days. But now I realize it means I can do what I want. I'm not really adrift, I'm sort of…free."

"So now you can pick out a house that's just right for you," Kate said. "Exactly what *you* want."

"Or…not at all." He let his words sink in for a moment. "What if the thing I've always thought I wanted wasn't really what I needed, after all? I always thought a permanent home would bring me happiness, but I realize now that I've had happiness for a long time."

Kate smiled. "You're happy with yourself, that's the best kind."

"Are you?"

Kate's smile faded and she physically drew back several inches. "Of course I am. I do what I want, go where I want. I'm not burdened by material possessions or what other people think I should do. I'm happy."

Her expression didn't reinforce her words, and Brady wished he hadn't killed her smile by asking, *Are you?*

Kate swallowed and glanced over at the fire station. "I should go. Your pizza is getting cold, and I never intended to stay long. I just wanted to say happy birthday and tell you I left a little gift for you at your house. Your brother can show you."

She started to turn away.

"Wait," he said. "Can I have a birthday kiss?"

Kate turned back to him, reached up and touched her lips to his, and Brady closed his eyes and tried to imprint her touch and scent so he wouldn't forget. He opened his eyes, and seeing her sweet face made him want to throw every bit of caution to the wind.

"I love you, Kate."

Her mouth opened and she took a huge step backward. She stared at him a moment, and then turned and walked toward her car as if a forest fire was chasing her. Brady watched her drive away, knowing he'd crossed a line but also knowing it didn't matter. The truth was the truth, and saying the words wasn't going to change anything. He loved her, and that meant he had to let her go.

When he got home that evening and saw Kate's surfboard leaning against the wall of his garage, he knew it was a sign that she was still planning to leave Cape Pursuit and the memories of their summer far behind her.

CHAPTER TWENTY-TWO

KATE WAITED PATIENTLY for about thirty seconds before blowing the trolley's horn. An expensive car with out-of-state plates was parked in the trolley lane, blocking the next stop. Kate's trolley was full of passengers who were temporarily enjoying the air-conditioned ride on the blistering August day, but they wouldn't appreciate a delay.

Despite three long blasts of the trolley horn, the sleek black sedan didn't move. Was there anyone in it or was it actually and unbelievably parked right in the way?

"Want me to get out and have them move it, or can we let people off here?" Josh asked as he came to the front of the trolley to see what the holdup was.

"I can't park on the street, it wouldn't be safe," Kate said. "Stay here. I'll see if I can get the guy to move the car so we can get into the stop."

Kate barreled down the three steps and approached the driver's window. A man's profile was visible despite the tinted glass. The window slid down, and a flash of recognition hit Kate. She hadn't seen him in over a year, not since the upscale wedding, but she was looking at her cousin's husband behind the wheel of the illegally parked car.

"Kate, oh my gosh, there you are!"

Her cousin Lillie flew from a boutique right by the car and ran toward Kate, waving shopping bags and smiling. "I knew you ran the trolley, so I told Cameron if we just followed the trolley lane, we might run into you. And here you are!"

Seeing her cousin was so unexpected that Kate stood, dumbfounded, in the street. Josh blew the horn on the trolley, and Kate swore she heard sirens approaching from a distance. If it was the police coming to clear the lane, she had better get Lillie and Cameron out of it.

"Lillie," Kate said, accepting a huge hug that included nearly being strangled with shopping bags. "What are you doing in Cape Pursuit?"

"Vacation," she said. "And then I saw this

amazing shop." She pointed behind her. "Have you ever been in there? It's all designer—local, of course—and mostly one of a kind. I got three skirts and—"

"You have to move your car," Kate said. The sirens were getting closer and she didn't want to contribute to a traffic incident. "I definitely want to hear about your vacation and see what you bought, but there's a city lot right around the corner. Park there. I'll pull the trolley into this space, and…we'll figure it out."

A fire truck blasted past them, and Kate caught a glimpse of Brady riding in the passenger seat. Brady, who had announced he loved her as they stood in front of the fire station on his birthday. And what had she done? Run away as if he'd taken a fire hose to her. Her wild idea from the night of Noah and Corrinne's wedding had flashed back to her a dozen times since Brady's impulsive words, and she'd tried to imagine the scene that had seemed so clear the night the search parties found the missing man. She thought she'd found something, too—a way to have her freedom but come home to Brady. But when she'd seen his face as he told her he loved her, she had panicked at the immense power of his words. He wouldn't accept a part-time relationship. That wasn't what he was looking for.

Kate watched the fire truck as it gained distance and tried not to imagine Brady going into a dangerous situation, even though she knew he did it every day.

"That was a close one," her cousin's husband said. "I was worried about the side of my car for a minute."

"Better hurry," Kate said, thinking a scrape down the side of his car might be a useful lesson for the future. Did he have any idea how hard it was to navigate these streets? Firefighters had a tough enough job. "And then come right back here," she told Cameron. "You can get on my trolley and I'll show you the sights while you tell me what's up with you and we get caught up."

Kate pointed out the city parking lot to Lillie's husband, and then Kate got back in her trolley. She grinned at the people seated in rows who were looking at her expectantly.

"Tourists," she said. "Can you believe those people?"

Everyone laughed, and Kate pulled the trolley into the stop and parked it safely before allowing anyone to get on or off. Before the last person disembarked, Lillie and Cameron were back and Kate ushered them into the front seat on the trolley.

"Do you mind driving?" she asked Josh. "I don't want to be distracted by my visiting relatives."

"No problem." Josh got behind the wheel, reached around to pull the bell and merged into traffic.

Kate took the microphone and gave an abbreviated explanation of the sites they were passing and route information, and then she sat across from Lillie and Cameron. "I can't believe you're here in Cape Pursuit."

"And I can't believe someone in our family finally tracked you down. You're the elusive runner in the bunch, worrying us all to death."

Kate laughed. "You make my life sound glamorous."

"I used to think it was," Lillie said. "When you left home right after high school to become a vagabond instead of a country-club wife, I was envious. I even told my parents

I was going to do the same thing as soon as I graduated."

"And?"

"And they expressly forbade it. Threatened to cut me off and told me no daughter of theirs was going to be a free spirit and tramp all over the country."

"Did they really say *tramp*?" Kate asked.

"Something like that. So I gave it up, did the smart thing and married this guy," she said, rubbing her nose on his cheek as he sat next to her on the bench. "And now we're here on a little beach vacation before Cameron has to fly to Europe for two weeks of meetings."

Lillie began describing their hotel—the most luxurious one in Cape Pursuit—and her shopping conquests so far on her trip, but Kate's mind wandered back to the month after her high school graduation when she turned down college, designer messenger bags, handmade leather boots for the coming fall, an expensive laptop and a chance to meet Mr. Right on campus. Her parents had been shocked and disappointed, there was no question of that, but they hadn't threatened her with disinheritance or come anywhere close to forbidding her from going her own way.

How hard that must have been for them, Kate realized now with six years of experience between her eighteen-year-old self and now. Each visit home since then, roughly every year and each time for some momentous family occasion such as a wedding, had come with a strong invitation to come home. They wanted her to give up what they called her reckless life on the road, but they hadn't tried to force her. She felt a shiver of guilt when she remembered what they said as she left each time. They had told her they loved her and wished she would stay.

"And the concierge desk is only open until six o'clock, so I want to get back to our resort by then so we can be assured of decent dinner reservations," her cousin Lillie was saying. Cameron was nodding politely but looking out the window at the passing scenery.

"Sure," Kate said. "This trolley is on the short tourist loop today, so we'll circle back around to your car in less than half an hour. That should give you plenty of time."

"And I'm making reservations for three so you can join us," Lillie said. "Unless it should be four?"

Kate shook her head. "Just me." Brady

might be available for the evening, but no way was she going to introduce him to her family. There were no firefighters in the Price family. Just investors, bankers, lawyers and the occasional tycoon. She wasn't embarrassed by Brady's profession, but she would be embarrassed for him to see firsthand what her family valued. If she was honest with herself, though, she knew the financial differences between her family and his was a lame excuse. How could she sit at a dinner table and make polite conversation with a man who'd confessed his love for her and to whom she'd given no answer in return? It wasn't something they could chat about while they waited for dessert.

"Your mother sent a gift for you," Lillie said. "When she heard we were coming to Cape Pursuit, she made me promise to see you, as if I hadn't already planned on it. I don't want to ruin the surprise, but I think it's a designer weekend bag. Maybe she hopes it will inspire you to come home. Everyone misses you, Kate."

"My parents could come themselves," she said.

Lillie shook her head. "Your dad has that

big project going on all summer and can't get away, and you know your mother would never set foot outside without him."

"I know," Kate said. It sounded as if nothing had changed, and it reminded her how lucky she was to have her freedom and go where and when she wanted. She didn't have to ask anyone's permission or opinion, didn't have to wait for anyone. If she wanted to pack her bag and leave Cape Pursuit tonight, there would be nothing stopping her.

Except…

And there wouldn't be anything she missed or regretted.

Except…Brady.

Josh picked up the microphone and informed the passengers of the next stop, and Kate jolted in her seat. She had been so lost in thought she forgot to do her job of talking to trolley guests.

"Your stop will be next," Kate said. "And then just text me the dinner time and location and I'll meet you."

"Are you sure you don't want to bring someone? Have you really been spending your nights in this gorgeous town alone?"

Kate shrugged. "Not all of them, but tonight I want to talk to you and hear all about what's new at the country club."

Lillie laughed. "They have a new chef they stole from New York City."

"Of course they do."

Kate waved to her cousin and her husband when they got off at the next stop. She was happy to have dinner with them, but she almost wished she had included Brady.

"WE SHOULD HAVE gone out on your actual birthday, but since we waited, we have two things to celebrate," Noah said.

"Two things?" Brady asked. They were seated at one of the nicer restaurants beachside, a place Brady had dined with Kate earlier in the summer. The clientele was a mix of families ordering sandwiches from the menu, couples on dates enjoying drinks and entrees, and singles at the bar.

"We think we found the right house," Corrinne said.

Bella clapped her hands and bounced in her seat. "It has a big tree I can climb."

Brady smiled at his niece. "But only if your dad climbs with you, okay?"

"That's the same thing he said," Bella said.

Brady nodded at his brother approvingly.

"You should have asked Kate along," Corrinne said. "She's probably leaving town soon, and I hate to monopolize your evenings when you'd probably rather be with her."

Brady sipped his drink. He doubted Kate would have said yes to a dinner invitation. Not after he'd blurted out that he loved her and she'd turned around and practically run away. Brady had checked the next week's trolley schedule, and he was relieved to see he and Kate weren't scheduled together. If he thought he could change her mind, he might try. But he couldn't ask her to change for him. Couldn't ask her to value four walls in the same way and for the same reasons he did. It was hopeless.

"Kate already has one foot on the road," Brady said. "And good for her. She has her future planned out, but it's not here."

Corrinne looked as if she wanted to say something, but Brady saw his brother give his wife a tiny nudge with his elbow.

"Can I have pop?" Bella asked. "I never get to."

"Only because it's a special occasion,"

Noah said. "And you have to brush your teeth extra before you go to bed tonight."

"I remember Mom saying the same thing," Brady said. "She was very serious about toothbrushing when we were kids."

"That's probably because she didn't have health insurance or any money for a dentist visit. It's amazing we survived," Noah said. His tone was light, but there was so much underlying truth that Brady felt the evening's cheerfulness get sucked away like water going down a drain.

"She loved you, though," Corrinne said.

Brady wondered how much Noah had told Corrinne about their childhood, and he had to assume it was everything. He couldn't have a five-year relationship with her, a child with her and a marriage without sharing his past. Brady had also shared some of his childhood stories with Kate, but not all of it. It wasn't that he didn't trust her. It was just that everything in his life that had driven him to want a home and security was the opposite of her life that compelled her toward freedom and a lack of ties. It was the story of their relationship—two ends of a string being pulled in different directions with no hope of meeting again.

"She did love us," Brady said. "However and whenever she could." He smiled and tapped his glass against his brother's. "And we turned out okay. At least one of us."

"Which one?" Bella asked, clearly not understanding the joke.

Brady, Noah and Corrinne laughed, and at that moment, Brady saw Kate across the restaurant moving toward a table with two people he'd never seen before. The loud laughter at his table drew her attention, and Brady and Kate locked eyes across the dining room. Kate stood next to her chair for a moment as if she was considering coming over to say hello, but then she sat down with the two other people. Her chair was sideways so Brady could see her profile. She looked beautiful, dressed up, her hair falling over her shoulders instead of being in a ponytail.

"You could go say hello," Corrinne said.

Brady's jaw tightened. Kate could easily have done the same thing. She was sending him a message by taking a seat instead.

"Have you told her how you feel about her?" Noah asked.

Brady let the question hang for a beat, but there was no use dodging it. "Yes."

The waiter came and listed off the specials for the evening, and Brady chose the first thing on the list so he wouldn't have to think about it. Instead, he was thinking about telling Kate what was on his mind. It would do no good, he knew that, but at least he'd know he'd tried. He wouldn't have to regret never saying the words in his heart.

"Be right back," he said, standing up.

Brady walked quickly before he could change his mind. He paused by Kate's table next to the empty fourth chair. Kate stood quickly, her cheeks flushed.

"Hello, Brady." She turned to her companions. "This is Brady Adams. He's a firefighter here in Cape Pursuit and he also works part-time on the trolley." He noticed all the things she didn't say, such as *Brady is my summer romance who recently told me he loved me.* Kate gestured to the two other people. "This is my cousin Lillie and her husband, Cameron. They're on vacation."

Brady shook hands with both people and exchanged some polite words, although he knew he wouldn't remember what they were in two minutes. He had a brief impression of smiling and well-dressed people, and he remembered a few of the things Kate had told him about her family. Expensive cars, weddings, houses.

"Do you have a minute to walk outside with me?" he asked Kate. He knew he was being rude, tearing her away from visiting out-of-town family, but his chances of talking with her were narrowing by the day.

"I... I..." she stammered, glancing at her guests.

"Just for a minute," he assured her, shooting a quick apologetic glance at her cousin. "I don't want to intrude on your time too much."

"Okay," Kate agreed. She followed him onto the boardwalk where there were dozens of tourists walking, biking and enjoying the ocean view. "Brady, I'm sorry I walked away from you the other night. I didn't know what to say, and—"

"It's okay. Maybe it was better that way because I was speaking impulsively, and now I've had time to think."

Kate's posture relaxed and her expression was relieved. Did she think he was going to take back his words, tell her that he hadn't really meant it when he said he loved her?

"I do love you," he said. "I didn't need to think about that. But I've been thinking a lot lately about my priorities. I've focused for years on finding a perfect house and then the perfect person and having a perfect family."

Kate's face colored again and she laced her fingers tightly together so the tips of them turned pale. Brady laid a hand over both of hers. "I don't mean to upset you. I owe you a lot for helping me realize I already had what I thought I was looking for. I already have a perfect family and a wonderful life, even if I'm renting half a house and my brother's family will soon get their own place. Even if I have an old pickup that smells like socks and tires."

Kate smiled. "And your fake pine-scented air freshener."

"Especially that." He put his free hand on her shoulder and fought the urge to hug her. His words would come so much easier with her in his arms, but her relatives were probably watching. His were, too, but they already knew how he felt. "What I'm saying is that love doesn't have to come with a street address and a two-car garage. Sometimes it's right in front of us."

"Brady, I—" Her voice cracked and her eyes shone with tears. "I'm not the one for you. You deserve someone who wants what you want."

"Let me decide that," he said softly. "What if I want you?"

Kate looked into his eyes and blinked back tears, but then she slowly shook her head. "This will never work. I'm sorry."

"Why not? Kate, I'm willing to make sacrifices to be with you, but there's one thing I'm not willing to do."

She waited, and he gathered his courage and went on.

"I'm not willing to give you up without a fight," he said. "I know it's not what I agreed to, but things have changed for me."

She held both hands in front of her. "Not for me," she said, her voice barely a whisper.

"Don't you see any way we could be together?" he asked, a note of desperation in his voice.

Kate squared her shoulders and walked back toward her table, taking the long route and weaving around the outside of the restaurant. Brady needed a long route, too, to compose his feelings. Twice he'd told her what she meant to him, and twice she'd walked away.

CHAPTER TWENTY-THREE

TWO DAYS LATER, Kate waved goodbye to her cousin as Lillie left town with her husband in their luxury car. Lillie and Cameron had ridden the trolley, which they called "quaint," taken a sunset cruise on a boat half the size of the one they owned at home and had one dinner and one breakfast with Kate. Most of their conversation was about Kate's family at home and who was getting married, divorced, having a baby, building a house or going on an expensive vacation. Lillie had asked pointed questions about Brady after Kate had returned to the table with flushed cheeks, but Kate had deflected her cousin's questions by describing Brady as a summer fling that was coming to an end.

That was what she said, anyway. The truth was that her heart was more involved than she wanted to admit, even to herself. She had never been in love because she had never allowed herself to be. The few interesting men she'd met over the past six years of traveling had been casual relationships. No commitment, no thought of them after she moved on. She had thought Brady might fall into the same category, but the fact that her heart had drawn her back to Cape Pursuit for a second season and then she'd agreed to a summer romance proved that there was more to it.

A lot more.

With each day working with him, spending time on the beach, having dinner, sharing stories, helping each other with friend and family issues, she'd gotten closer to Brady. She thought of him when she woke up in the morning and when she lay in bed at night thinking about her day. He was part of the sunrise over Cape Pursuit and the soft ocean breeze. He was part of her summer.

Was it more?

Kate walked toward the trolley office where she was training one of the other summer workers to take over the paperwork. Dinah had agreed to stay on after the summer ended and try to fill the role of office manager, but there were so many moving parts that Kate knew it was going to be a tough job for anyone to manage.

There had been a few moments in the training so far when Kate thought she might be making a mistake by choosing to turn down the job and leave Cape Pursuit. What if she stayed and spent more time exploring her relationship with Brady, seeing the house he would buy, walking through autumn leaves with him?

Her phone rang, and she dug it out of her purse. Brady. She swallowed, holding the phone in her hand, and stared at his name on the display. She was afraid to answer it because she felt vulnerable and very afraid of the powerful realization that she might be in love with him. *In love with him.* The phone stopped ringing and the display announced that she had a voice mail.

Hi, it's Brady. I know we've sort of...hit a wall in our relationship, but you only have a week left in Cape Pursuit, and I'd like to see you. I'm working at the station tonight, but maybe tomorrow if you can? Thanks. There was a long pause, but Kate waited because the message still had ten seconds left on it. *I care about you, Kate, and I don't want to say goodbye, but if you have to go, I want us to part on good terms.*

She wanted that, too. It was how she operated. Part of not having ties to people and places was knowing when and how to leave. Without loose ends or hard feelings, nothing left on the table. Her family was different. They would always be a tie and there was plenty left on the table. Each time she thought of them, it cut into her freedom and reminded her how easy it would be to settle in and be owned by them, their fancy houses, their inviting lifestyle.

It would also be easy to let herself be loved by Brady. Too easy. But there was no way it could work. He was bound to Cape Pursuit, and she was ready for the adventurous career she wanted.

She texted one word to Brady. Tomorrow.

Kate worked in the trolley office all day, went home and took a short nap, and then signed herself into the driving app for the evening. Friday nights were big money with tourists enjoying the nightlife. With all the extra shifts she had picked up and with the scholarship offered by the flight attendant school, she had enough money now to pay tuition and living expenses. Everything she wanted was right in front of her for the taking.

Her first Uber riders of the evening were low-key. Two sisters in town with a seniors' bus tour wanted to meet an old friend for dinner on the other side of town from their hotel. Kate gave them her number for when they were ready to return later. She picked up a family next who had stayed late at the beach and were anxious to get the kids in the bathtub and order a pizza straight to their room. The parents were too exhausted to talk, and the kids smelled like sunscreen and wet hair. One of them fell asleep on the short drive to the hotel, and her soft sweet cheeks reminded Kate of Bella. She would miss seeing Bella. What would her first day of preschool be like?

"Beachfront Motel," a young man said as he got in the back seat.

"Which one?" Kate asked.

"I requested a driver, not a comedian." The man was about her age, wearing a button-down shirt that was untucked and had a stain on the front. His face appeared flushed when the interior light of her car came on, and his words were sharp and slurred at the same time.

Kate blew out a sigh. "How about an address?"

"Don't you know where you're going?" he asked.

"I'm afraid you don't. Maybe you should get out and request a different Uber," Kate suggested. "Someone you might be more confident with."

"Jeez," the guy said. "You don't have to get all crabby." He showed her his phone, which had his hotel reservation information on the screen. "I don't need another driver, now do I? Besides, you're prettier than most of them. Probably."

Kate took a moment to consider her options, but she decided to risk it. He was in the back seat, obviously intoxicated, but it was a short fare. She would drive him across town and drop him off and maybe she would call it a night after that. Although she had always loved driving, she was starting to lose her enthusiasm for it. Would she have to deal with belligerent people on airplanes? She grimaced as she looked in the rearview mirror and pulled out into traffic. At least she wouldn't be alone with strangers on airplanes.

One time at a truck stop on a dark night in the middle of Oklahoma, a man had followed her from the restroom back to her truck. Luckily for her, a highway patrol officer had just pulled in and she walked straight to his car and talked with him until the other man got in his vehicle and left. She had gotten by on her wits for six years, but she had to admit she was a little tired of it.

"You're cuter than I thought when I first got in," the man said. "Maybe you could come in and have a drink with me at my hotel."

"Can't," Kate said. "I'm working."

She drove a little faster, hoping to get rid of her passenger before he made an utter fool of himself.

"Almost there," she said.

She turned off the road along the Atlantic and pulled up in front of a mostly deserted-looking place. It wasn't one of the nicest hotels, off the main tourist route and closer to a residential section not far from the fire station.

"I don't think this is it," the man said. "Why don't you drive me around a little more so I can talk you into that drink?"

Kate's pulse quickened, but she wasn't going to let him frighten her. Her mind raced, thinking of ways to get him out of her car, preferably someplace where other people were around.

Brady. He was working at the fire station.

"I'll take you for one loop around the neighborhood," Kate said. She pulled out and drove one block to the fire station. It was a warm evening, and all the outside lights were on. The doors were up revealing shining trucks, and three firefighters were playing basketball under the floodlights.

Kate pulled up directly onto the concrete apron, interrupting the basketball game. She jumped out of the car, aware of the surprised looks from Brady and the two other firefighters. Brady took one step toward her but paused. Kate jerked open the back door of her car and said, "Out."

"What the heck? Hey, lady, this isn't the hotel."

Brady moved closer, his shoulders squared, hands fisted, but he didn't interrupt.

"Your hotel is one block that way," Kate said, pointing. "Get out of the car."

She could see that Brady was practically vibrating with anger, but he still didn't move. Kate could have married him at that moment—a thought she didn't even want to try to process. He was there for her, but he was letting her do things her own way, trusting her.

The drunk passenger leaned out the door, saw the three huge firefighters and then stumbled as he climbed out of the car.

"That way," Kate reiterated, pointing again.

"Jeez," the guy said. "I'm not paying for this ride."

He started to walk away, clearly unsteady, but he still turned around and gave Kate a mean look.

"Want us to go after him and rough him up a little?"

Kate laughed at the stocky firefighter who made the offer. "You wouldn't do that."

"Probably not, but it's fun to think about."

Two of the firefighters went inside, but Brady stayed, his feet planted and arms across his chest.

"Thanks," Kate said.

"I didn't do anything."

"I know. That's what I'm saying thanks for."

Brady uncrossed his arms and ran a hand through his hair in an exasperated gesture.

"You're trying to kill me, right? If I had to watch that guy give you a hard time for five more seconds—"

"But you didn't," Kate interrupted. "You trusted me to handle it."

"It felt wrong as hell, but I'm guessing it was…right?"

Deep sorrow settled in where the adrenaline left a vacuum inside her. She'd wanted Brady's help and protection, but that was the problem. It was time for her to leave before she gave away any more of herself, her independence to a man who wanted all of her.

"It was right," she said. "You're a great guy, Brady, and I know you're going to be really happy. You'll get that house and a promotion, all the things you deserve."

He blew out a breath. "This sounds like a big goodbye coming no matter how much I want—"

"I can't stay," Kate said.

Brady ran a hand over his face, exasperation showing in every gesture. "You didn't give me a chance to finish, Kate. You're so sure you know yourself, and so sure you know what I want, but I don't think you do. I wasn't going to say I wanted you to stay."

She swallowed. "You weren't?"

"No. I was going to say I want you."

Kate took a long, slow breath of the night air. It was now or never, and her next words would change everything. But...her mind was already made up, her choice the one she had been heading toward for years.

"I have the next two days off, and I'm going to drive down to Florida and finalize my housing arrangements."

"And then?" he asked. An alarm went off inside the station, and Brady cocked his head to listen. Lights flashed on. A truck engine caught and roared.

"You have to go," Kate said.

Brady started walking backward toward the station. "Come back and say goodbye before you leave for good," he said. "Please."

Kate didn't answer. Instead, she got in her car and drove it quickly out of the way of the emerging fire trucks, tears running down her cheeks.

EARLY THE NEXT morning, Kate packed everything in her Escape. It only took her an hour to remove all traces of her occupancy from the summer apartment. Avoiding entanglements, possessions, relationships had left her free, and the sparse loads of clothes and possessions she hauled out to her car reminded her how much she liked moving on. She put on her road trip playlist and drove straight through to the airport in Florida where the housing director, Linda, was still at her desk late in the day.

"You're lucky," Linda said. "The girl who was in your apartment left last week."

"Did she graduate early?" Kate asked.

"No," Linda said. "She discovered she didn't like flying as much as she thought."

"Oh," Kate said. "She didn't know that in advance?"

Linda shrugged. "I guess not. Some people, huh? Either way, the place is empty and you can start moving in anytime."

Kate thought about her car full of possessions. She'd taken a chance that there would be a place to store them for a week, and she'd gotten lucky. Was it a sign that it was meant to be?

Linda handed her the keys and gave her directions, and Kate drove to her home for the next several months. She carried in three boxes and two laundry baskets full of things and plunked them down inside the door. She had everything with her. It would be very easy to call George and ask him to mail her last paycheck and give her remaining three trolley shifts to someone else. The season was almost over, and the other drivers would probably be happy to pick up the work.

Maybe Brady would pick up the shifts and put away the extra cash for his house. Kate sank into a chair in her new apartment's kitchenette. The place was like a lot of the temporary spaces she'd occupied over the years, a few months here, a few there, always just a stopover on the way to where she was going. The freedom was almost suffocating.

CHAPTER TWENTY-FOUR

BRADY SPENT THE next four days kicking himself for not coming up with the right words
to convince Kate they had a future together.
He let the first two days go by, hoping he'd
have another chance when she came back to
town one more time.

But then George had called him and asked
him to fill in a shift. He hadn't even asked
whose shift it was. He knew. Kate was gone
and she wasn't coming back.

"You busy after work?" he asked Charlie
on the fifth day.

"No," Charlie said with a grin. "A guy like
me with two jobs, a wife and a daughter is
just looking for ways to stay out of trouble."

Brady smiled for the first time in days.
"Sorry. Any chance we could take another
look at that house? I think I'm ready to make
a decision."

"The blue one on Vine Street?" Charlie
asked.

Ethan leaned against a truck and crossed his arms. "You're still buying a place?"

"Of course I am," Brady said, his tone defensive. "I mean, that was always the plan."

"I know," Ethan said. "I just thought you got a little distracted this summer."

"I'm back on track," Brady said. This was the first step he knew he needed to take. His brother's family was getting their own place, he was signed up for professional courses that would lead to a promotion and—he swallowed the pain in his throat—Kate was gone and she wasn't coming back. He needed to make the right choice for himself.

"It almost sold last week," Charlie said, "but the buyers decided at the last minute they didn't want to put any work into it, not that it needs a lot."

"I don't mind the work," Brady said. Physical work would keep him busy, keep his mind off the long summer days that had been filled with false promises.

"Meet you over there about four," Charlie said. "I'll let you in, but I can't stay long. Jane has a city council meeting tonight, and I get our daughter all to myself for the evening."

Brady parked in front of the house with the

big tree and the blue siding, the one he'd seen
with his brother and niece. He smiled thinking about the pink bedroom Bella had liked.
Maybe he would leave it pink for when she
came to visit. It could be a playroom for her.

"You're serious about this, aren't you?"
Charlie asked.

"Ready to sign the papers," Brady said. "I
just want one more look."

"Go ahead," Charlie said.

Brady walked through each room, flip-
ping on light switches, bouncing a little on
the hardwood floors where there was a creak-
ing sound under his feet. He turned on the
kitchen tap, opened and closed cabinets and
tested the view from the living room window
into the backyard. He had known it when he
first saw the place. It could be home.

He tried to ignore the bittersweet feelings
that crept in when he considered how much
sunnier the rooms would be if there was
someone there to share it with him, but he
owed himself the fulfillment of a dream. He
owed himself the chance to make this house
a home.

"I called the seller," Charlie said, coming
in from the front yard, "and told them they

could expect a contract in the next day or two. Hope that's okay."

Brady nodded.

"I've got to get going," Charlie said, edging back toward the front door. He tossed a set of keys and Brady caught them one-handed. "Lock up when you leave, and I'll catch up with you tomorrow about that contract."

"Are you sure that's okay?" Brady asked. "I can leave now if you want me to."

"No," Charlie said. "Take your time. I'd trust you with my own house keys."

"Thanks," Brady said, waving to his friend. He went into the backyard and stood over the pool, watching the water circulate a green leaf around its surface. Brady leaned on a tree and looked toward the house. His house—almost.

A flash of movement inside caught his eye. Had Charlie returned? Brady shoved off the tree, but then he stopped dead. Kate Price opened the back door and stepped outside into the late-afternoon sunshine. She smiled hesitantly and looked uncertain—something Brady had seldom seen in her expression. Had she come to finally say goodbye for good?

"I stopped by the fire station," she said as she came toward him. Brady wanted to go to her and take her in his arms, but he had to let her say what she had come to say. Even if it was goodbye. He glanced up at the solid roofline of the house, trying to take courage from the tangible lines of it, the home that would be his soon. "Ethan told me where you were."

Brady nodded.

"This is a nice place," Kate said, stopping just in front of him so they were both in the shade of the tree. "Beautiful."

"Thanks. I'm making it official."

Kate bit her lower lip. "I set up my place in Florida. Moved everything."

Brady felt any glimmer of hope leave his body. "I'm glad you came back to say goodbye," he said, even though he almost wished it hadn't been at the house he was buying. He'd never stand under the tree and look at the back door again without wishing Kate would come through it.

Kate put a hand on his cheek and her fingertips caressed the hairs just over his ear. The feeling was pure heaven and hell at the same time. If she was going to break his heart and leave, he should encourage her to do it fast. Rip off the bandage.

"You know I left home because my parents treated me like a princess, right?"

Why was she telling him this? He already knew her reasons for not getting involved and getting tied down. Unless…something had changed? He began to feel the tendrils of hope coming back even though he knew he should be cautious.

"And you found out you made a terrible princess?" he asked, trying to keep his tone light until he could get his feet under him again.

She dropped her hand and cocked her head at him. "Being perfectly dressed, coddled and groomed to be someone's perfect wife was no life for me."

Brady lowered his voice to a near whisper. "What is the life for you, Kate?"

"Making my own choices."

He nodded. "I know, and I do understand." They were back to where they were, but at least he knew the stakes and knew he had already lost the game.

She drew a deep breath. "Making my own choices also means deciding who I want to be with. Who I give my time and my heart to."

Brady held his breath.

"I decide who I fall in love with," Kate said.

Brady put a hand on his chest. "If it's not me, tell me right now before I pass out from lack of oxygen."

Kate smiled. "It's you."

"You love me," he said, not daring to believe it.

Her smile vanished. "Don't you believe me? Am I too late?"

Brady pulled her close. She put her arms around him and laid her cheek on his chest.

"Never too late. I told you I never give up on people. I love you, too, Kate." He ran his hands over her back, relishing the feeling of her against him.

She sighed. "You smell like tires and campfires."

"Sorry."

"It's wonderful."

He kissed her temple and then his lips moved across her cheek and found her lips. Her lips were so tender and sweet under his, and he felt for the first time as if the place he was standing was home.

"What changed your mind?" he asked. "When you left, I thought you were gone for good."

"Leaving Cape Pursuit and starting over in a new place didn't come with the same thrill it used to. And it should have. I always move on, enjoy my freedom, am excited for the next thing. But this time, I realized I was giving up something I could never replace. I couldn't give you up, Brady."

"I'm glad. You have no idea how much."

"I don't know how this will work," she said. "With you living in Cape Pursuit, and me flying—"

"I don't need to live here," Brady said, shaking his head. "I told you last week, I finally figured out that happiness doesn't have to have a postal address. I haven't bought this house yet."

"But you need a house," Kate said.

"I need you," he said, his hands cradling her cheeks.

"But I need a house," Kate said. "I've never had one of my own."

Brady was trying to keep up, but his head was spinning. Kate laughed. "I can't work all the time. I'm going to go to airline school in Florida for a few months and get my training, and then I'm going to get the job I've always wanted."

"You should," Brady said. "You deserve to go after your dream."

Kate smiled. "I don't think I'm making myself clear. I'll blame it on the fact that you're a wonderful kisser and it distracted me."

"I could give you another sample of my skills," he offered.

Kate laughed. "Here's my plan. There's an airport an hour away in Norfolk where I can fly out of for work. I already checked. It won't be international flights so I'll miss out on that part of the scholarship, but I have enough tuition money, and I'm happy to stay in one country. All I'm missing now is someplace to come home to at the end of the day."

"Someplace to come home to," Brady repeated slowly.

"And someone."

Brady held her tight and felt her cheek flex against his. She was smiling.

"Does this mean we're definitely splitting the grand prize if one of us wins?" he asked.

"We talked about it earlier this summer, but it will sure be easier if we're together," Kate said.

"I love this plan," he said.

Kate looped both arms around his neck

and reached up to touch her lips to his. "How about a tour of your new house?"

"Our house," he said. He wrapped an arm around her waist, and they went inside the sunny house with the sky-blue siding where the soft creaks under their feet were swallowed up by their laughter.

* * * * *